M. AINIHI

Rise

A Blood Inheritance Novel

Acknowledgements

I want to thank my husband, and the rest of my family, who supported and encouraged me to make this book a reality.

A special thanks to my editor Allister Thompson. Rise could not have been written to its fullest without your professional advice and assistance.

To all the freelancers I have had the opportunity to work with on The Blood Inheritance Novels, including but not limited to, artists, illustrators, graphic designers, cover designers, various editors, and logo designers you have my deepest gratitude. It is an honor to be able to work with so many talented individuals from around the globe.

Cover Designs © rebecacover
Interior Illustration by Tauseef Ahmed
Editing by Allister Thompson

i

Prologue

Erol could still hear his mother's words echoing in his head.

She had eyed him wearily. "Have patience," she said in her soft voice. "Being allowed passage through the planes is a privilege."

Erol hammered the ground with his fist in frustration and pushed the dark hair away from his forehead.

He scooped up the pages he had been reviewing and held them up into the sky, waiting for a gust of wind to steal them from his grasp. As the pages began to flutter in the breeze, he released his hold and allowed them to be carried away into the fields.

He had studied the human plane and its culture tirelessly. *There are already jinn younger than me allowed to pass into the human world. I'm ready—why can't they see that? Instead I'm stuck here babysitting.*

Erol plucked the blossom from one of the bright red flowers that littered the valley, pulling out its palm-shaped petals one at a time, as his charges chased each other back and forth through the grass without a care.

A decision should have been made by now.

The ground around him was littered with the flowers large, delicate pieces, and he frowned at his handiwork, suddenly unsettled by the way the bright red petals surrounded him.

A shadow overhead brought him to his feet. Erol studied the cloudless blue sky, looking for signs of danger. The mountains that enclosed the valley seemed to sparkle and shimmer in the bright sun as if encrusted with emeralds.

Erol counted the youngsters as they darted around, many changing shape even as they moved, not yet having found their true form.

Satisfied that everyone was accounted for, he returned to his thoughts.

His mother just didn't understand, couldn't understand; she was content to remain on the spirit plane, surrounded by the magic of the mountains. There were many legends of good and bad humans, and likewise many legends of good and bad jinn. He had studied them all. Erol restlessly awaited the day when his own story could begin.

He crossed his arms in front of him and again verified the number of younglings, his dark brown eyes squinting in the harsh sunlight.

Erol glanced toward the thatched-roof homes in the distance. He sighed in relief and allowed his arms to fall to his sides. Someone was finally approaching on the worn dirt path from the direction of the council meeting.

Erol took a deep breath to calm his nerves and slowly began following the children. "Hey, wait for me," he yelled as they flocked curiously toward the cloaked being.

The man stopped walking as the children circled him playfully. The being looked directly at Erol with haunting gray eyes. Erol's stomach knotted. *That is no council member.*

Erol ran toward the children in desperation.

The man pushed his hood back and made a gesture in the air. Erol tried to call to the youngsters again. His throat seemed suddenly constricted, and only a raspy squeak came out. His body would no longer move forward. It felt as if his legs had rooted themselves to the ground.

Too late, Erol realized the intruder's ill intent; he watched helplessly as the strange man reached out and grabbed one of the younger boys while chanting something Erol could not understand.

All remaining hope left Erol then. There was only one language hidden from the jinn: the secret language of the Arcane. Beings created with the sole purpose of destroying the jinn race.

The sorcerer wrapped one arm around the child and raised a stone dagger. Runes on the blade glowed brighter and brighter with each phrase spoken aloud.

Erol tried to call to the villagers with his mind, but that, like the ability to speak aloud, seemed to be affected by whatever incantation the sorcerer had used.

Within a fraction of a second, the strange man and the young jinn were gone.

Erol sank to his knees. His heart pounded with the fierceness of a war drum, and his hands trembled. *How could an Arcane being have entered our realm?* After all, the magical races had been separated by the goddesses into individual realms to keep things like this from happening. *No.*

Erol shook his head slowly back and forth. They were separated to keep the humans away from the never-ending feud that had almost caused their extinction.

The surrounding air sparked, crackling with the energy of frightening magic that he had only ever heard about in legends.

His punishment for failing to keep the youngsters safe would be immediate.

He did not try to resist as the magic engulfed him.

He had proven himself unworthy.

The world went silent as Erol was thrust into darkness.

1

Amanda opened her eyes before her alarm even sounded. She flung her bed covers to the ground, tied her long blonde hair back, and dressed quickly.

She snuck down the stairs and peered into the kitchen. Her father sat at the table with his back to her. Steam rose from a mug beside his arm; a newspaper was spread open in front of him.

Amanda held her breath as she slowly tiptoed closer.

"I know you're there," he said, barely glancing up.

"How do you always do that?" she asked as she sat across from him and rested her head on her arms, trying to be dramatic.

"You're not as stealthy as you think you are," he said as he turned the page.

Amanda sighed.

"And you try it every weekend," he added, winking at her over the top of the pages. "You better eat something."

"I can't eat, I'm too excited." She always looked forward to Saturday. "Where are we going this week?"

"It wouldn't be much of a surprise if you knew, would it?" He shuffled the pages.

Amanda grabbed a pear from the fruit bowl. "I am fifteen. Maybe I have outgrown surprises," she said, nibbling at the pear.

"My daughter? Never," he said, setting the paper down. "It's a long drive. Remember, be ready…"

"…for anything," she finished, smiling. "I have to grab my pack," she added as she turned to the closet.

She closed the passenger side door and sighed. "How can it be a surprise if you use the GPS?" she joked.

"Funny," he said as she buckled herself in. "I turned the sound off, no peeking."

It was tough not to glance at the destination, but Amanda kept herself occupied by watching the scenery as they drove away from the busy university town where she had lived with her father since she was a baby.

An hour later, the smooth asphalt changed to dirt and rock, and the small car bounced up and down as her father drove over deep ruts and through mud puddles. Endless fields stretched out in the distance on all sides except directly in front of them.

They fast approached what appeared to be a solid brown and green wall of spruce and hickory.

At the edge of the dense woods, her father pulled the car off the dirt road. He looked around the area, frowning. "Hmm." He scratched his head, a hint of concern in his voice. "They say it's one of the best trails."

Amanda hopped out of the car and grabbed her gear. "I'm sure it's amazing."

Her father pulled a map from the back seat. "Let's see, the entrance should be right about there," he said, pointing a few yards away.

"Well, get your stuff, let's go see," Amanda said as she pulled at his arm. "It will be great." Her father always put a lot of thought into their weekly adventures, and she enjoyed spending the time with him. She did not want him to think that she was disappointed.

The trail opening was overgrown and threatened to close in completely. Branches poked at them as they walked through in single file. Twigs and leaves crackled beneath their feet. Her father held the map tightly in his hand. "A little more this way, I think," he said as he veered off to the right at a fork in the trail.

It's so peaceful here, Amanda thought as she breathed in deeply, enjoying the smell of pine.

The trail began to open up more as they got farther in. Her father stopped to stuff the map into his pack and hung a camera around his neck. "That's better. It looks like we have the trail to ourselves." He winked. "Let's see what kind of trouble we can get ourselves into."

Woody vines snaked across the trail, threatening to trip them up as they pointed out interesting plants and searched for animals hiding among fallen trees and in bushes.

"Isn't that a paintbrush?" Amanda asked, pointing up a hill where the sun had managed to peek through the canopy.

"Castilleja," her father corrected as he looked at the tall, slender, brightly colored plants.

Amanda wiped the sweat off her brow and sipped from her bottle of water. Even in the shade of the woods, it felt like it was nearly eighty degrees. "Isn't that a prairie flower?" she asked, wondering how it came to be growing here in the forest.

"Usually," he responded as he veered further off the path and headed in its direction for a closer look.

Amanda followed, careful to keep her eyes out for poison ivy. One encounter with that plant had been enough for her.

Her father stopped halfway to the top and appeared to be petting a tree. Amanda rolled her eyes and laughed. "What are you doing?"

"This tree has something carved into it. Come here and check it out." His blue eyes gleamed. "These symbols look almost familiar," he said, scratching his head.

Amanda knew he loved a good mystery. She figured it reminded him of the past, when he would travel to archaeological sites and participate in digs for the university.

She adjusted her pack and continued to wade through the brush. The craggy-looking tree defiantly stood out from the rest. The other trees stretched skyward and were thick with leaves and needles of widely varying intensities of green. They looked majestic. This tree was barely taller than her father's six feet and completely devoid of leaves, full of knuckles and branches that were crooked. *It looks like it belongs on display beside a haunted house.*

"Creepy," Amanda whispered.

"Beautiful," he replied as he traced the strange shapes carved there with his finger.

"That probably just means old, spooky tree," Amanda joked. But he didn't laugh as he walked around the tree, snapping photos.

Amanda shrugged and continued to explore the perimeter. A flash of white out of the corner of her eye caught her attention.

Had something bolted up the hill? "Probably a rabbit," she said aloud, knowing her father wasn't really listening. She didn't mind; he had given up many things for her, and she wouldn't deny him his fun. She hoped one day he would be able to go back to the life he had left behind for her, instead of being stuck in a classroom all day.

Eager to make her own discovery, she continued up toward the sunlight.

As Amanda neared the top, peculiar stone pillars became visible. There were five in all, spread out in a circle. *Perhaps they are the foundations of a small building?* she wondered.

In their overgrown surroundings, the freestanding stone pillars looked magical to Amanda. Dew-covered flowers and vines twisted around the structures; they appeared to sparkle as the sunlight rained down on them.

Amanda stepped back and slowly circled the outer perimeter. *The center isn't very large, maybe twenty feet across.* The pillars themselves only rose a few feet above her. *Maybe seven or eight feet tall*, she guessed. *What kind of stone building would be in the middle of the woods? Maybe it's older than the forest?*

Amanda trotted toward the strange structures, wanting to get a closer look before she shared her discovery with her father.

Her foot hit something hard hidden among the vegetation, and she let out a startled cry as she stumbled forward directly into one of the pillars. Her hands shot out, stopping her head from making contact.

"Amanda?" her father called after her.

"Yeah, I'm okay. You should come see this, but watch your step," she added, eyeing the large, moss-covered stone that she had tripped on.

Amanda's father remained silent as he trudged up the hill and began to walk around the outside of the pillars, studying them. He reached for his camera, and as he adjusted the lens, Amanda saw something shimmer in the grass near the center of the circle.

Excited to make another discovery, she hurried into the center toward the thing that poked out just above the grass and weeds. Amanda crouched to inspect the buried object...

"What you got there, Mandy?"

Amanda grimaced at the nickname. "I'm not sure yet." She had secretly hoped he wouldn't notice her digging into the earth but was relieved when he didn't rush right over. She watched him for a moment as he continued to occupy himself by taking pictures of the stones and occasionally jotting in the little notebook he kept in his pocket. It had always been his habit to document everything.

As the rest of a shiny metallic handle emerged, Amanda tried to yank it up out of the earth, but it refused to budge. Determined to get it out on her own, she dug her fingers in deeper. Dirt built up under her nails as she tried to extract the object from the earth's tight hold.

After several minutes of digging, Amanda's fingers started to ache. She sat back on her heels to examine the object. She had managed to uncover most of what looked like a golden teapot. It looked different from the one they used at home. Above the rounded bottom rose a long slender neck. At the top, the pointed lid seemed to have been fused shut.

Afraid that she would break off its skinny, twisted handle, she gripped its neck with both hands and gave it a hard tug, grunting with the effort as she pulled.

"Shoot," her father cried out.

Amanda released the object and looked up, just in time to see him fall forward into one of the pillars. "I told you to watch your step."

"No harm, this is pretty sturdy," he said as he smacked the structure with his hand, causing the pillar to lean to the side.

Amanda swore the earth groaned in protest, even before the ground beneath her trembled with the impact as the pillar came crashing down.

Amanda watched, frozen, as her father scrambled away, just as the next pillar started to fall. It sounded like thunder in her ears as the structures collided. The ground shook violently with the next impact. She felt the earth buckle beneath her, then just as suddenly she felt nothing beneath her. She screamed and shot her arms upward toward her father as she slid down into the darkness.

2

Amanda could feel the cold, damp earth beneath her. She sat up slowly; a deep throbbing echoed through her skull, and she winced as her hand brushed against a raised bump on her forehead.

It was pitch black. Pain shot through her tight, sore muscles. She ran her hands over her arms and legs, pleading with them to loosen up.

She needed her backpack; there were always a few essentials in it. A small first aid kit and compass. The flashlight, of course. Not that she ever remembered using it for hiking before; it just always had seemed like a good idea. Sunscreen and bug repellent, she wouldn't be needing that right now. One Ziploc bag with matches and a pocket knife. There were also a few granola bars and a bag of dried apples. And last but not least, three water bottles. *It must have slipped off during the fall.* She went to her knees.

Her muscles screamed as she made sweeping motions with her arms, feeling for the pack. She hoped the batteries in her flashlight were still good. Her hand brushed the rough canvas strap, and she let out a breath of relief. She pulled the bag toward her and began to riffle through the contents. As she gripped the cylinder handle, she almost smiled.

She pushed the switch and a beam of light shot out, casting

its glow only a few feet in front of her. Lifting it above her head as far as her arm would reach, she searched for the place she had fallen through; she could see only the same solid wall of darkness. *The hole must have filled in above me as I slid down.*

She shined the light along her arms and legs, looking for damage; gray, chalky dust layered her skin and clothing. Other than the lump on her head and sore muscles, she seemed unharmed. She redirected the beam of light toward her feet and found the ground was covered in the same chalky dust. She shouldered her pack, not wanting to lose track of it.

Amanda walked slowly forward until a wall of gray stone came into view. Running her hand along it, she followed the wall until she came to the first corner and then the second. She forced herself to walk on, verifying that she was in fact surrounded by four solid walls. *No way out.* Her heart began to race as she realized she was trapped.

She slid back to sitting position, propping herself against the hard stone wall, and placed her pack between her legs. *Breathe, just breathe, this is no time to freak out, breathe.* She took slow calming breaths, like her father had taught her to do when she would wake in a panic after a bad dream.

Her father, *yes*, he had seen her get swallowed by the earth. He would get help. Someone would be coming to the rescue, but it could take hours for them to get to her. Amanda knew she just needed to keep herself calm.

Her heart rate slowed, but her head was still pounding. She pulled the pack open and felt for the small first aid kit inside. She tore the packet carefully and placed the capsule between her teeth as she unscrewed the cap from one of her water bottles. Her throat stung as the liquid washed the capsule down.

She remembered that she had left her cellphone and purse

locked in the car. Not that it mattered. She doubted she would get service down here. Not really hungry, she nibbled halfheartedly at a granola bar and sipped some more water.

Amanda didn't hear any noise above her. The complete silence was unnerving. She decided to pass the time by trying to figure out how big the basement was. Carefully, she walked back around, counting heel-to-toe steps. She soon lost track as her mind started to wander.

She imagined what would happen if whatever was holding the dirt in place shifted and everything came down on her head while she stood there waiting. Would they ever find her in the rubble? Had her father actually seen her fall down into the earth? She tried to remember if he had left his cell in the car, as she had.

Her foot hit something that made a metallic sound as it skittered a little way ahead. Shining the flashlight in the direction of the noise, she saw the treasure she had been digging for. It looked more like junk to her now than anything else. She reached down to pick it up and carried it back over to the pack, holding the flashlight in one hand as she turned the object in the other, studying it.

Tiny symbols covered the object, but some of the creases were filled in with dirt. She couldn't ever remember seeing a teapot before with such elaborate designs carved into it. Amanda stuffed it into her pack, knowing she shouldn't waste water trying to clean it now. *They should be coming any minute.* It already felt like it had been hours, but she knew that couldn't be true.

Amanda propped herself back up against the wall. Realizing it might be a good idea to conserve her batteries, she thought about turning off the flashlight. She giggled nervously at the idea. "A little old to be afraid of the dark," she whispered to herself.

The idea of turning off the light made her skin crawl. A chill ran down her spine as she looked out into the darkness beyond the faint beam of the flashlight. She knew it was crazy to be afraid of something coming at her in the dark. There were definitely four solid walls all around her, but it felt like the darkness was going to close in on her at any moment. Amanda hugged her knees to her chest.

Her eyes started to well up. She felt the first one slide slowly down her cheek, no doubt leaving a streak on her dirty face. She couldn't stop them as they came faster. Her nose started to run. She wished she had a tissue. That just made her cry harder. She continued crying into her knees until her eyes felt puffy and swollen.

She tried to wipe her face with the back of her hands and took a few sips of water from one of the bottles.

"Someone will be here at any moment," she whispered, as if that would stop anything lurking in the dark from coming at her.

"There's nothing down here but me and dirt," she reassured herself, hoping that saying the words out loud would make a difference. It didn't. She had goosebumps on her arms. She couldn't shake the feeling that there were a million eyes watching from the dark that surrounded her. Amanda pulled the little knife from her backpack and opened it. It was only a few inches long. She tested the blade against her finger. It felt sharp. She knew it couldn't do any real damage, but something was better than nothing. Somehow, she eventually managed to doze off, holding the knife in one hand and the flashlight in the other.

When she opened her eyes, it took a moment to remember where she was. Darkness surrounded her once more. She had dropped the flashlight and knife. Her body broke out in a cold sweat as she felt the ground for the objects. She jerked back in pain and let out a scream as something bit into her hand.

She scrambled to her feet, shaking slightly from the attack. She held the wrist of the throbbing hand with the unharmed one as if it were going to fall off at any second. Amanda kicked her foot in the direction from which she thought the attack had come.

She heard the clink of metal against stone. Realizing she had cut herself with her own knife didn't make her feel much better. Again she got down to feel across the floor for the flashlight.

She remembered the matches in the Ziploc bag. She knew if she lit them there would only be a few seconds to look around. It seemed kind of wasteful. "What if the batteries are dead in the flashlight?" *Great. Now I am talking to myself again.* She rolled her eyes. Alone in the dark for a couple of hours, and she already felt like she was losing her mind.

She decided that if she just lit one at a time, it would be okay. After all, there was always the chance it would only take one. Feeling around in the pack for the plastic bag, she thought of the first aid kit.

"It won't do me much good if I can't see." The sound of her own voice somehow made her feel more confident in her endeavor. Carefully opening the bag, she pulled out the little box of matches, hoping it was the right way up so that all the matches would not fall out when she slid it open.

Luck was on her side; she struck the first match on the side of the box. "Tragedy avoided," she said aloud. "After all, someone will be here really soon," she reassured herself again just as the first match went out.

Striking the next match, she searched desperately, keeping low to the ground. The flame barely dented the darkness. As it fizzled out, Amanda held her breath and reached for a third. She paused, temporarily frozen as a scraping noise came from every direction at once.

Her hand was shaking as she struck the third match too hard against the box and it snapped in half. *How many do I have left?* she wondered, holding her breath as she struck the fourth match. As the flame appeared, she exhaled.

The flashlight was right in front of her. As she reached for it, the scraping noise grew louder. Her heart pounded so hard, it seemed to echo in her head.

Amanda flicked the switch back and forth. Nothing happened. She screamed in frustration and let it fall at her feet. The scraping noise ceased.

Frantically, Amanda reached into the bag and searched for something, anything that would help. Feeling the smooth wrapper of a granola bar, she tossed it to the ground without hesitation.

Something began falling onto her face and hair, startling her. She reached up to feel the grainy substance. Amanda didn't have to see to know that it was dirt from above. Terrified, she was sure the ceiling was going to come down on her head.

She didn't think her state of panic could get any worse until the scraping noise resumed. She was scared, angry, and alone. She grasped the metal object that had caused all of this. Letting the bag fall to the ground and taking the artifact in both hands, she hurled it as hard as she could into the darkness.

The room was filled with bright light. Amanda's surroundings shifted and fell away. The walls themselves seemed to crumble out of existence.

"I'm dead," she whispered, squinting to see in the harsh light.

"Not yet." The deep voice seemed to come from all around her.

"Where am I?" her voice quivered.

"Everywhere and nowhere," he replied.

"What's that supposed to mean?" The light was fading. Amanda swore she could almost make out a form in front of her as her eyes fought to adjust to the changing light.

3

Tony's feet were sore from pacing back and forth for hours as he waited to be reunited with his daughter. "It can't be empty. I know what I saw." His head was pounding as he stared down into the empty hole.

He had dug at the surface, pleading with the soil to part ways, until his fingers grew painful and then the dull ache subsided, and they were numb from the action.

"What I am saying is that there is nothing down there. It is a completely empty stone cellar. There is no sign that your daughter was ever there." The rescue worker rubbed the back of his neck.

They had been digging for hours to unearth the cellar. It was a slow process. They didn't want the whole thing to come down on Amanda. It seemed the debris had been stopped from collapsing completely by just a few odd roots and stones that had filled in the opening in just the right way.

Tony noticed a mud-smeared name tag pinned at a crooked angle on the rescue worker's bright orange vest. Just the *Ji* was visible; the last half was fully encrusted with the mud. Tony clenched his fists, trying to keep his temper at bay as the rescue worker closed his eyes and took a deep breath.

"You said yourself when the structures fell, you turned and ran away from them. Isn't it possible Amanda turned and ran into the woods?" He was trying to calm the father; he needed his help to find the missing girl.

"Jim?" Tony questioned, eyeing him for approval. "I saw the ground swallow her up." His voice rose steadily with each word, until he was practically yelling. "I know what I saw." He threw his hands up in frustration and stalked a few feet away.

Tony knew he was being the typical distraught parent, the worst people to have to work with. He didn't care; it was becoming increasingly hard for him to concentrate.

"She left her cellphone in the car," Tony continued, his voice shaking.

Jim nodded. "Yes, you did tell me that." He waved his arms, motioning to the surrounding forest. "You said she was no stranger to the outdoors."

"We go hiking now and again, even take the occasional camping trip, but she is no expert on survival in the wilderness," Tony said as he peered over the caution tape into the basement below. It was completely empty, just as the man had said. He wasn't as relieved at the sight as the rescue workers had been. He had been here. He had seen her get sucked into the ground and then the ground fill back in above her.

"Okay, I need to get these people organized into teams to look for her in the woods. I think maybe you should go wait for her at the entrance just in case she finds her own way out." He motioned a man a few feet away to come over.

"Take him back with an ATV to wait at his car. I think that would be best for now." The man nodded and led Tony toward the four-wheeler.

Tony felt like he was in a daze. He was still trying to come to terms with what had happened. He had lost her. His daughter. The only family he had left. He didn't say a word as they drove back out to the parking lot. His head was reeling, and there was a strange tightness in his chest.

An ambulance was parked by his car now, along with a few other vehicles. Some of the rescue workers' cars, he guessed. One of the EMTs tried to ask him if he needed assistance, but he shrugged him off.

Getting into his car, he locked the doors and rested his head on the steering wheel. There was nothing left to do but wait. As the pounding in his head subsided, his skull was filled with a new sensation, one he could only describe as something picking at his brain.

Amanda could hear her name in the distance. Faint light trickled down from the trees above her.

"Amandaaaaaa," several unfamiliar voices called. "Ammandaa."

She lifted her head from the ground, swatting some leaves out of her hair as she sat up. Amanda tried to answer the calls, but her mouth felt like there was a whole bag of cotton stuffed inside it.

Her pack was on the ground, where she had been lying, with half the contents strewn about. Reaching out for the bottle of water a little too fast, she was assaulted by vertigo.

"Ammmandaaa." The voice already sounded farther away.

Amanda brought the water bottle to her lips and drank.

"Here," she croaked out. She cleared her throat to try again. "Here I am."

She felt her eyes dampen as her rescuers came into view. Someone threw a blanket over her shoulders and lifted her into the safety of their arms. Relieved, Amanda hugged the man's shoulders tightly, clinging to him as he carried her out of the woods.

The rescue was a blur. Amanda barely realized she was in an ambulance until they were unloading her at the hospital. The doctor had asked questions she couldn't quite understand as he examined her, concluding that she was physically as healthy as a horse, other than the egg-shaped lump that had receded slightly and the cut on her hand that was now cleaned and bandaged.

Amanda was glad no one asked how she had gotten it; she

didn't want to explain the craziness that she had let run rampant while she was lost. She covered her head with a blanket; she couldn't even remember how she had made it back out of her underground prison and into the woods.

When she had told the doctor about her loss of memory, he waved it off. He reassured her that she was just in shock and referred a psychologist she might consult after discharge. He had further explained how confusion and loss of memory were quite common in the type of situation she had been in. Secretly, Amanda doubted that most people would have become irrational so quickly. But she had nodded and thanked him.

Before they sent her home, the doctor came in again and reassured Amanda and her father that she would be her normal self in just a few days. "Be sure to get some rest," he added before hurrying away to his next patient.

She had spent the first evening home with the light on in her room all night, jumping at any sound from behind the closed door.

Amanda lay there trying to think, straining to remember. *Three days. How could I have been missing for three days?*

After the darkness, all she could see, no matter how hard she tried, was bright, harsh light.

Enough! Amanda threw her blankets to the floor and jumped out of bed. The water of the shower seemed to literally wash her worries away, and she emerged ready to get back on track. After pulling on her favorite worn jeans and a T-shirt, she looked at herself in the mirror. The bruise on her forehead had almost completely faded, and the lump was gone. She peeled the bandage from her hand to see all that remained of the cut was a thin, scabby line. She headed downstairs, still brushing out her mass of wet blonde hair.

4

As Amanda rounded the corner into the kitchen, her father jumped slightly, and Amanda couldn't hold in a giggle as he fumbled with his coffee cup. "Sorry, Dad."

"Feeling better today, I take it. Good. I have to go into work." Setting his coffee cup on the counter, he massaged his temples.

"Are you feeling okay?" Amanda asked as she skulked over and gave him a hug.

"Just a headache," he said as he grabbed his briefcase.

"Have a good day at work," Amanda said, picking up the empty pain reliever bottle from the counter where he had discarded it and tossing it in the trash.

"You take it easy, Amanda," he said seriously. "The doctor said you need to rest."

"I feel fine." Amanda smiled. "But I promise no heavy lifting or big construction projects."

He scowled at her response but glanced at his watch and headed out the door.

Amanda grabbed an apple and went back up to her room for her laptop. She was curious to see if there were any interesting articles about her time in the woods. She typed in "Amanda Garrett" and added the words "lost" and "missing."

All she could find were a few small paragraphs from some of

the area papers. *Of course,* she thought, shutting the top, *they can't write a whole article if they don't have anyone to interview.*

There had been a few requests, but how could she tell them about her survival in the woods for three days if she didn't have the answers to give? *I could tell them what I think I remember, but that would just lead to more questions I can't answer.*

Amanda picked up her cellphone and pressed the "on" button. The phone sounded like it was possessed as it beeped and vibrated, signaling that a barrage of messages had come through. Amanda thought about how she would respond to the questions her friends would ask.

What was it like? Her skin prickled. A giant coffin. Were you scared? No, I was terrified. How did you get out?

Amanda decided to ignore the phone and turned it back off. She sat on the edge of her bed, not sure what to do. She spied her backpack resting against the closet door.

She didn't remember taking it from the woods. *One of the search and rescue team must have grabbed it. Did they bother to collect the scattered contents, though?* Amanda picked it up and dumped it on the bed. Sorting through the objects, she selected the pocketknife and eyed it suspiciously, sure she had left it in the cellar.

She continued picking up each object gingerly and looked at them in turn. Everything seemed to be there, although the matchbox was empty and the flashlight was cracked. *Did I imagine the basement the whole time? Did I run into the woods like a maniac and survive for three days alone?* Amanda didn't think so. *How did I survive, and how did I get out of the cellar?*

One object remained that seemed out of place. She brushed the antique lightly with her fingers to make sure it was really there. She shook her head in disbelief, remembering throwing it fiercely into the darkness.

Picking it up by the handle, she carried it down to the kitchen. The spout was full of some solid gray substance. Amanda filled a large bowl with warm water and some detergent and immersed the object. Leaving it there to soak, she went to get a rag and spare toothbrush. This wasn't the first time she had tried to clean up some old thing they had found while exploring.

Hunched over the object, Amanda meticulously cleaned the strange design, slowly working the toothbrush into and around the intricate engravings. She had never seen a design quite like it. She was mesmerized by the detail and didn't want to take her eyes off it as she reached out for the rag and polish, knocking the bowl of water off the counter. Amanda let out a shriek and jumped, and the artifact dropped to the floor with a clatter as she scurried for the mop.

Cursing, mop in hand, Amanda froze as she rounded the corner, her eyes locking onto a stranger. He made no move, just stood there appraising her with his deep brown eyes. Amanda heard the clank of the mop handle hit the floor. She took a step back.

"You're afraid of me?" He looked at Amanda skeptically. "That's rich." He scoffed. Amusement filled his gaze as he studied her.

As the initial shock wore off, Amanda reached for the phone that was usually in her pocket, only to remember she had left it upstairs. Panic seized her, and she turned to flee from the stranger. Her foot went down onto a wet spot and slid, causing her to fall backward. She closed her eyes, anticipating the pain as her head met the slick floor tiles.

Instead, Amanda felt firm hands grab her, stopping her inevitable descent. She opened her eyes and was met once again by those deep brown eyes. They seemed familiar to her, but she couldn't quite place them. "Why run from me, Amanda?" the stranger asked as he released his grip. He stood several inches above her, and Amanda could see ripples of muscles under his red T-shirt. She could feel her face get warm. He looked at her quizzically, causing goosebumps to form on her arms with his gaze. "You summoned me, after all."

"How do you know my name?" Amanda stammered, again backing up from him, this time careful to step away from the spill.

"I know a few things. Goes with the territory." He sounded more amused by the second. He stepped toward her and Amanda backed up another step to feel the hard edge of the table press against her, trapping her all over again. She could practically see the darkness of the basement folding in on her. Her legs felt wobbly beneath her.

A smile spread across his mouth. He chuckled as he took a few steps backward. "You really have no clue, do you." He shook his head and clicked his tongue.

Amanda took a few deep breaths and relaxed a little. *He's not here to hurt me.* Although it seemed that he definitely had been toying with her for his own amusement. Walking around the table, he bent down to pick up the artifact she had been cleaning and set it on the table. "This," he said, pointing at the now-shiny gold object, "is my prison, which you apparently unwittingly summoned me from again."

Amanda squinted her eyes. "You said prison, as in jail?" He seemed so young. Not much older than her, and yet his eyes told a completely different story. *A person could get lost in those eyes.*

He cleared his throat, breaking her trance, and she looked away. "That's not important. What is important are rules. There are rules that cannot be broken by me, and you need to know them.

Do you understand?"

"Not really, no." Amanda shook her head.

His brow furrowed and anger seeped into his face. "I am from the race of jinn, or genie if you prefer. I'm sure you have heard of a genie. Why I was imprisoned is no concern for you. You summoned me here, and I am here to fulfill your requests, as is required by my sentence." He spat out the words as if they left a bad taste in his mouth. "Oh, mistress, what can I do for you, silly girl," he taunted.

"Leave the way you came," Amanda responded, not believing a thing this lunatic had said. *Why did I even indulge in his wacky fantasy to begin with?* she wondered as she watched him walk to the door and turn the handle. Sighing, Amanda went for the house phone. She wanted to call the police, even if the situation had been defused. Not hearing the distinctive sound of the door opening and closing, she turned back. But the stranger was gone.

5

"He was wearing faded jeans and a red T-shirt," Amanda said to the man in blue sitting at her table sipping tea. He seemed disinterested.

"So let's see if I have this straight. A young man with dark brown eyes and brown hair came into your house uninvited. You said he was several inches taller than you, making him what, about six feet and muscular. He stopped you from falling, had a conversation, and then left. Nothing was stolen or broken. Is that it?"

He doesn't believe me at all. Amanda could see it in his face and hear it in his voice. *I can't tell him I think he is still in my house.* The officer obviously already thought she was making it up.

Amanda's father rushed inside just then, offering his hand to the officer, who stood and accepted it. They spoke in hushed voices for a few minutes before the officer glanced over at Amanda and shook his head.

"Uh-huh," was the only discernible word Amanda could make out before he covered his thinning gray hair with his hat and left.

"Dad..." Amanda started as the door shut behind the police officer.

He interrupted. "Amanda, I explained that you had recently been through a lot, and he is willing not to press charges for your false statement."

Her jaw dropped. "I wasn't lying, Dad."

His ears turned red with frustration. "Amanda, enough, go to your room."

Bewildered, Amanda did as she was told. *I have never lied to my father. He has always trusted me before.* She lay on her bed and wondered how and when she had lost that trust. Confused, she drifted into a restless sleep.

Amanda awoke to thunder that seemed to make the house shake with every crash. The sky was dark, but the window illuminated every few seconds as lightning flew through the air outside. She walked to her window and pushed it open to peer out. The wind blew debris around in the street. She could feel her shirt getting damp as she stared into the sky, counting the seconds between flashes.

As the strikes became more frequent, Amanda knew that it meant the storm was not moving away, but closer. She reached out to close the window as the sky lit up again, illuminating a face outside. The mouth was open in a wide grin right in front of her. Her heart jumped in her chest.

Amanda turned and made a mad dash out of her room, slamming the door behind her. She pressed her body against it, as if it would keep the thing from getting to her.

Amanda could feel her heart racing; her hands shook slightly from the shock of what she thought she had seen. She looked down at her dry shirt. Amanda stood still. She no longer felt the house shuddering or heard the crashing thunder. *A dream, it was a dream. Did I just sleepwalk then?* She took a few deep breaths and moved away from the door, shaking her head at herself in disbelief. *When did I become so jumpy?*

She headed down the stairs for a glass of water, pausing as she heard faint voices coming from her father's study. Amanda approached it slowly, gently pushing the door open with her hand.

Her father's head rested in the crook of his arm. He was snoring softly atop a mountain of papers. The golden artifact she had found stood on the corner of his desk. Amanda wondered when he had brought it in here.

She walked around the desk. The voices were coming from his computer monitor. A crude video someone had probably taken with their cellphone was playing. It was the first day of the search, when they had attempted to dig her from the earth, only to find she wasn't there at all. Amanda watched as they tediously scraped at the surface until finally breaking through. Shouts of approval could be heard just as the picture turned white and started to replay from the beginning. Amanda questioned why he had been watching it. No doubt he had already seen it a hundred times.

"Dad?" she called softly, lightly shaking him. His eyes opened, and he yawned. "You fell asleep," she said obviously. He shot up with a shocked look and ushered her out of the room, closing the door behind him as he exited.

"You should go up to bed," he said, not looking at her.

Amanda complied, and he followed behind her up the stairs until he saw her go into her room. Amanda listened until she heard his door close, then waited about ten more minutes to be sure he was asleep. She tiptoed back down to his study. He was acting weird, and she wanted to know why.

Amanda had never felt like she needed to sneak around her own house before, and it was unsettling. Quietly she closed the door and sat down at his desk.

He had left the video up on the screen, and she watched it again. She didn't notice anything unusual. She scanned the papers on his desk. A few were notes and pictures from the hike. Some pages were covered in writing she could not recognize. Others were pictures of a strangely decorated dagger. The designs engraved on the blade were almost identical to the ones from her treasure. Amanda examined the pictures more closely; with the exception of the shiny silver hilt, the dagger appeared to be made from some kind of stone. Next to the dagger in the picture was a sheath covered with jewels and the same type of writing that was on the papers.

Beside her golden relic was a magnifying glass. Picking up both to take a closer look at the designs, Amanda was disconcerted. She bit her tongue to stop herself from yelping as a pale mist seemed to rise from the spout. Amanda released her grip on it and moved back. Her mouth gaped. The form that solidified in front of her was the same young man on whom she had called the cops.

"You look surprised to see me." He smiled.

Amanda closed her mouth and cleared her throat. *You're still asleep, this whole thing is a weird dream.* That would have explained a lot. Amanda pinched her arm hard and then tried to rub the pain away with her hand.

"Are you ready to talk now, Amanda?" he asked, looking around the room. The color seemed to fade from his face. "Where did you find that?" he snarled, pointing to the pictures on the desk.

"I, it's something my father was looking at." She was frightened once again. "This is his study; I don't know what those are."

He furrowed his brow. "Amanda, that thing is dangerous. Does he have it?"

She shook her head. "I don't think so, no." His face softened. *He believes me. Well, at least someone does.*

28

He took her hand and pulled her in closer. "Are you sure?" Amanda looked into his eyes. Her heart fluttered in her chest at his warm touch. As he let go of her hand, her head seemed to float back to earth.

Amanda blushed and turned away, embarrassed. She had some crushes when she was younger, but nothing serious. This pull that he had on her felt a hundred times stronger than anything she had felt before.

Amanda suddenly wanted him to disappear again. Here she was standing in her pajamas in the middle of the night; her face felt hot. She couldn't take his stare anymore. She had the feeling he knew exactly what he was doing. She sucked in a deep breath, gathering courage. Prepared to scream, she quickly whipped back around to face the direction where he had been. Once again he was nowhere to be seen. Shaken and confused, Amanda picked up the artifact and trotted up to her room, closing the door behind her.

Lying on her bed, she put her pillow over her head and released the scream. *This is insane. I am going nuts.* She had to be. *It's the only explanation.*

Grabbing her laptop, she searched the word "genie." Nothing useful or even related came up other than some pictures from animated movies of a blue genie rising from a lamp. Was that what she had, a magic lamp? Searching the word "jinn" yielded slightly better results. They were supernatural spirits of mythology that possibly resided in a different dimension. There were many different theories and ideas. After clicking a few links and reading a few paragraphs, Amanda gave up on that approach. She never did much like searching online. It seemed the answers she wanted would have to come directly from him. *Unless he is a figment of my imagination.* It dawned on her that she hadn't even asked his name.

The sky was beginning to brighten with sunlight. After throwing on some fresh clothes, she went into her bathroom, only to come face-to-face with him. She rolled her eyes and pushed past him, annoyed, to the front of the sink. "What are you doing in here?" she whispered as she picked up her toothbrush and squeezed some paste onto it. Lifting it to her mouth, she paused. The teenage boy, now standing behind her, cast no reflection in the glass.

"I am real, Amanda."

Shrugging off his statement, she brushed her teeth as if he wasn't there. She continued on to her hair and noted her forehead, which was now just as pale as the rest of her skin.

She spun quickly around as if to whack him with the brush, saying, "Do you mind?" But he was no longer there.

"Sorry," her father replied from the bedroom doorway, sounding startled and offended by her reaction. "Your door was open. I just wanted to let you know I was heading out. No surprises today. Please." He turned and tromped down the stairs before Amanda could respond.

The jinn materialized beside her, causing her to jump. *I will never get used to that.* "Can you do that anytime?" she asked, thinking of when she had been changing before. A smug look appeared on his face.

"If you're insinuating I would watch you when I should not be, you are mistaken. But yes, I can choose to be seen or not." This statement made her a little uneasy. Amanda wanted to know when he was around.

"Promise me you will not wander around here all invisible, please."

"As you wish, mistress, but I did not think your father would like to see a strange male in your room." His statement was true enough. Amanda wasn't sure how her father would have reacted. But she didn't want to find out either.

"Please stop calling me that. My name is Amanda, as you are already aware." She crossed her arms in front of herself. "What is your name, anyway?" She cocked an eyebrow at him as she said it.

He smiled in response. "You can call me Erol," he said, bowing slightly.

"Well, Erol, I think you can go find someone else to bother." Amanda immediately regretted saying it.

He glared back intensely. "It's not that simple, Amanda. You called me from the lamp. We are now linked until death do us part. Whether we like it or not."

"Wouldn't my father have also summoned you?" she questioned. "And what do you mean until death?" This talk wasn't helping her feel better at all.

Erol took a seat on the floor as he explained. "It works on a first come, first served basis, dearie." He motioned for Amanda to sit, but she resisted. "I can only have one master at a time." He winked as he added, "Anyway, you're better looking than he is."

Ignoring the compliment, Amanda gave in and sat.

"Death," he continued, "to state the obvious, means until one of us dies."

"You mean when I die. Aren't you immortal or something?"

"No, you have been reading too many of the wrong kind of stories." He glanced knowingly at her computer. "I can die almost as easily as you. Especially in this form." He gestured to himself. "I am also allergic to iron, so please refrain from wearing any."

Amanda had a question on the tip of her tongue but was afraid to ask, and she found she didn't have to. "No, Amanda, I cannot read your mind. But we do have an emotional connection. If you are frightened or nervous, I will feel it." The playfulness in his voice had vanished again, and he stared down at the floor, appearing lost in thought.

Afraid he would disappear again, Amanda asked the first thing she could think of. "So do you grant wishes?"

Erol looked up at her, shaking his head. "Not exactly. I mean, I can help you. I guess I'm more of a guide than a wish granter, per se." He fidgeted with the strings of the shag carpet beneath him. "Let me see, how can I explain? Jinn were created to be more than what humans are."

Amanda furrowed her brow and shifted uncomfortably.

"That's not what I meant." Erol stood and began to pace the room. "We, the jinni or fire spirits, if you prefer, were given elemental magic at the time of our creation, which allows us to travel with the wind or choose to be seen or unseen by humans. There are other things too..."

Amanda looked back at him blankly.

"Okay, mythology aside, the long and the short is I can do things humans don't have the ability or talent to do. Therefore, I am or should be useful to you in some way."

"You're not very good at explaining this," Amanda said.

"I wasn't saying we think we are better than humans, I'm saying that's what our creator intended. It doesn't make it true. In fact, some jinn work very hard to be allowed to pass into the human realm. It's an honor."

"But for you it's not. It's a sentence."

Erol shook his head. "To be here isn't the sentence. My sentence is to be bound to my prison and my master." He stopped pacing and looked down at Amanda. "Never to be completely free." He turned his back to her. "I'm going to leave you alone now for a while." Then he was gone.

Amanda quickly grew restless alone in the house. She attempted to reach out to a few friends on the phone, but no one picked up. *What would we talk about anyway? Erol?* She didn't think so. *My lost in the woods experience?* She still didn't want to go there either. Boredom and curiosity got the better of her, and she went back to her father's study to snoop.

Amanda's stomach growled as she looked at the documents again, and she realized she hadn't eaten that morning. She had been chewing on a pen in frustration. There was no indication of where the new pictures had come from. Giving up, she pushed herself away from the desk.

She quickly made a sandwich in the kitchen and gobbled it down. "Errool." She called his name experimentally. "Are you here?" Looking in each of the rooms downstairs, she saw no sign of him.

He met her on the way up. He didn't look thrilled. "Yes," he

said. "I'm up here where you left me." She was confused yet
again by his statement.

"You left me, remember."

"No," he corrected. "I can only go so far from my prison. If
you want me at your beck and call you will need to keep it close."

Amanda didn't want to go out alone; she still had this over-
whelmingly uneasy feeling. But she couldn't stay in another
moment. "Come out for a walk with me," she demanded, feeling
a little ashamed to be so pushy. She wasn't sure what had come
over her. *Fear, mostly,* she thought. The doctor had told her it
would pass eventually, but she wondered.

Grabbing the lamp from her room, she threw it in her backpack
and shouldered the bag.

Erol was silent as Amanda led him out of her suburban home
and down the quiet street. Children laughed and in the humid
heat. A few dogs barked and wagged their tails as they passed by.
The sun felt great on Amanda's skin; she had been inside way
too much the last few days.

"Erol?"

He looked at her quizzically. "How do you look normal, I mean your clothing and stuff?" she asked in a hushed voice, blushing as she said it. He stopped walking for a moment and shrugged.

"Amanda, you're trying to understand something that's not meant to be understood." He took her hand and made a motion with his over it. A palm-sized black diamond appeared there out of thin air. It glittered in the light. "It's magic; it is not meant to be categorized and theorized," he said, closing her hand around the stone.

He continued walking. "Black diamonds are said to grant courage and can amplify energies." Looking at his feet, he continued. "Also, it is said they allow a person to look within without illusion." With that, his form shimmered and disappeared from her sight.

Amanda knew Erol was still there but felt apprehensive as she clutched at the thing in her hand. She paused and looked at the stone. It was exquisite, and yet the hairs on her neck prickled as she studied the gem. She swore she felt it hum and vibrate with energy. Amanda slid the diamond into a pocket in the front of the backpack, eager to be rid of the feel of it on her skin, and wiped her hand across her jeans as if it had become soiled by the object.

"Even a thing that appears to you out of thin air has to come from somewhere," she whispered to herself as she headed back in the direction of her home. Suddenly she wanted nothing more than to curl up in her bed and hide like she had done the first day after she came home from the hospital. She just couldn't remember what she was hiding from.

6

Warning bells were going off in Amanda's head as she approached her home—something was not right. The front door was wide open, daring her to enter. "Erol." She choked out his name. Amanda wasn't sure that she wanted to go in without a solid person at her side.

Erol materialized beside her and took her shaky hand as they crossed the threshold together. Amanda let her backpack slide off her shoulder and crash to the floor as she stood and looked into the house.

The refrigerator door was hanging open, and milk was dripping onto the linoleum from a tilted carton. Normally neat and orderly, it appeared that a micro burst had found its way in through the front door.

Furniture was overturned, and papers were strewn about everywhere. They found the drawers in her father's office had been emptied, the contents scattered. Glass littered the carpet where a picture of Amanda and her father had been knocked to the ground and shattered.

Every room in the house was in the same shape. Nothing of value seemed to be missing, at least nothing Amanda could see right away.

Remembering the way her father and the officer had acted the last time she called the police, Amanda was sure not contacting them would be the right choice. She realized telling her father that she had left against his wishes was not the best way to gain his trust back. She was, after all, supposed to stay home and rest.

As if he could hear her thoughts, Erol began setting the house to rights, and she soon followed suit. They saved her room for last. Nothing had seemed to escape the blast. Her laptop lay on the floor, the case cracked. Amanda wondered if she should tell her father she had dropped it. Clothing had been thrown everywhere. The shelves in her bathroom were bare, and the contents of the bottles lay in puddles on the floor.

With Erol's help she lifted her mattress and set it back on the bed frame. A picture fluttered out, landing on the rug. Amanda could not recall exactly why she had hidden it, but it had been in that same spot for years. She guessed it was her way of keeping her mother close.

The blurred photo had been given to her by her father, teary-eyed as he recounted the day he had taken it.

In the beginning, Amanda had listened enthusiastically to the stories, bewitched at the idea of love at first sight.

Standing in a desert village, under the heat of an unforgiving sun, his crew had been hard at work digging, and he had been photographing the landscape for both his records and his own pleasure.

He said he had lifted the camera to his face and snapped the shot without ever realizing she had entered the scene. As he lowered the camera, he was met by a tall blonde woman, something you didn't encounter often in the far eastern parts of the world. She was a vision of beauty, wrapped in a loose brown dress.

She had smiled at him and told him he needed to leave, and he had smiled back and asked her on a date.

When Amanda was young he would end the story at this point rather abruptly, but of course as she became more curious with age, she had begged relentlessly to hear the rest.

Hesitantly, he began to reveal more details. He warned Amanda that forbidden romance never ended well, and theirs would not be an exception.

So as she grew, the story evolved, with her father adding in bits of information as he felt she was mature enough to better understand the situation.

This woman, Fatin, his enchantress as he called her, had been asked by the local people to come to the town specifically to rid them of his crew. They were able to keep their relationship hidden for some time, long enough for Fatin to know she was going to have a child.

This she managed to hide carefully, but as the crew continued to work and the townspeople continued to grow skeptical, they threatened to send her back from where they had summoned her.

Fatin urged him to stop his crew from working, afraid the people that had appointed her would revolt. He did as he was asked, and Amanda had been born in secret. Scared for the safety of her child, with a tear-stained face she had begged him to take their baby and not look back.

Tony had pleaded with Fatin to return with them, but deep down, he said, he had always known she could not. She had many obligations, and it would simply never be permitted. In the end he had done as she asked. The only thing saving him from complete heartbreak had been the infant that he brought back with him.

He had named her Amanda after they returned to his homeland. He requested a teaching position at the university, and after some time one was made available. He had never returned to the field, and as Fatin had requested, he had never tried to track her down.

It wasn't until after he had been forced to return to his home that he had discovered the image of Fatin, a smile forever plastered on her face.

Amanda thought the flaw in the photography that caused her mother to have red eyes only made her more beautiful, and she cherished the picture, the only thing that she had to remind her of the mother she had never known.

Her father often told her she looked just like Fatin. Amanda hoped it was true.

Amanda stuffed the photo into her backpack. Each time her father spoke of Fatin, sadness and longing filled his eyes.

Amanda wished that she had known her more at this moment than ever before. She would never admit that to her father; she wouldn't want him to ever think that his love wasn't enough.

Exhausted, she lay on her bed, staring up at the ceiling. She counted the stars that she had hung up when she was about ten.

A few had come loose and fallen, but the majority remained, and if the room was dark they still glowed faintly. That glow had always somehow been comforting to her.

Even with Erol's help, cleaning up the mess the intruder had left had taken hours. Amanda yawned and rubbed her eyes. Erol seemed to take the hint and made himself scarce.

The backpack that was propped against the closet door once again contained three treasures, two of which Amanda thought she would never want to part with.

She hadn't told Erol about the uneasy feeling she had gotten while holding the diamond. She assumed he must have felt it too, if they were in fact connected emotionally. Trying to push the creepy feeling away, she looked at the stars and imagined herself sitting outside under them. Maybe next to a glowing campfire to stave off an autumn chill.

The tree in her dream was familiar; it reminded her of the tree from the forest. Although it did not seem so creepy to her here, it appeared to have the same strange shapes carved throughout. Instead of being completely barren, the crooked branches were covered in white and pink flowers that dared to bloom even though the ground was covered with a shimmering layer of frost. It stood not in the heavily wooded area she remembered, but as a lone tree surrounded by wildflowers of all colors. They peeked out above the frosted, icy-looking blades of grass, set in a field that seemed to stretch out for miles in all directions. Frigid air blew at her exposed skin. She heard her name riding on the wind all around her. Just a whisper, but she had heard it all the same.

Shivering and rubbing her arms, she looked around, frantically trying to find the source. She searched the field with her eyes. Amanda noticed a patch of ground in the distance where there was none of the crisp, frozen, knee-length grass. It formed a circle. The few flowers that leaned into the circle looked singed, as if there had been a small fire there. She looked harder at the spot, squinting. The wind whispered her name again.

Green eyes stared back in her direction. They did not seem to be looking at her but past her. As if they could see through her. A young man now knelt in the circle, his long, dark hair partially hanging in his face as he looked forward. His eyes looked sad, his lips pressed into a straight line. Chains bound his hands in front of him.

Discovering that she could not find her voice to respond, she tried to move her feet. They seemed to be stuck to the ground. Amanda wanted to help him, but it was just a dream and there was nothing she could do.

A rustling that seemed to come from beneath her startled her.

As Amanda looked down at her frozen feet, the frosty spirals of icy crystals grew longer, twisting upward, causing a tingling, numbing sensation throughout her limbs. Wherever they touched, her skin grew a faint blue as they snaked up her legs, wrapping and twisting around. She gasped as it made its way to her torso, and she could see her breath as it escaped her lips.

Amanda awoke safe in her bed. Her heart pounded in her chest. Erol was standing over her, his eyes wide with worry.

As she sat up, still shivering, her teeth chattered uncontrollably. She clutched her blanket around her, trying to bring back some warmth.

Erol didn't speak as he put his arms around her. His touch felt like fire on her frostbitten skin, but Amanda made no move to stop him. She just sat there silently trying to absorb his warmth.

Erol did not seem to mind. He didn't ask about the dream. Amanda thought maybe he didn't need to.

7

Pots and pans could be heard banging in the kitchen downstairs, and Amanda realized her father was home. *Is it the weekend again already?* She carried the backpack with her as she descended the stairs. It was already becoming a habit for her to take it everywhere she went.

Tony smiled up at her from his hunched position. "I thought maybe pancakes. We can stay in this weekend while you continue recuperating." He stood up with the griddle in his hand. "Honestly, Amanda, do you think reorganizing the whole house was necessary?"

Amanda had hoped he wouldn't notice. "Sorry, Dad, I was bored." *Well, at least it was only a half lie,* she thought. *I was bored before I went out for my walk.* The silence as they ate bothered her. Amanda had never had trouble talking to her father about anything before. She only picked at her food as he perused the paper.

Amanda hadn't heard him go up to his bed last night. She noticed the dark circles under his eyes and wondered if he had also been having bad dreams, or if maybe falling asleep in his study was becoming a habit.

As he turned the page, a brightly colored flier fluttered out and landed on the table. Amanda picked it up with slight curiosity. The advertisement was for Oolas's Antiques; the grand opening, it seemed, was today. It boasted having rare and wonderful artifacts from all over the world and beyond. Amanda giggled at the last part, and her father stared over the paper at her for several moments. She was starting to feel uneasy about the look in his eyes; he didn't just look tired, he looked irritated and strained.

He set the paper down and his lips curled into a strange smile. Amanda had never seen a smile like that on her father's face, and she wasn't sure what it meant. It looked almost forced. "Maybe you have been in the house too much after all," he said as he rubbed his stubble-covered chin with his eyes glued to Amanda.

Amanda hadn't remembered ever seeing her father without a clean-shaven face. She wondered if maybe she was driving him crazy now as well as herself.

"Sure, Dad, where to?" He pointed at the flier, and his strange, twisted smile seemed to stretch even farther. Amanda tried to tell herself that it was her own imagination as she peeled herself from the chair to get ready to go.

"Are you sure you entered the right address?" Amanda asked as she looked at the rundown brick building in front of them.

A small wooden sign squeaked as it swung back and forth on rusty hinges. Stopping it with her hand, she could see that it did indeed say "Oolas's Antiques" in swirling cursive, just as it had on the flier. The door had been left propped open by an old wooden crate.

"I thought this was the grand opening; it looks like this place has been here for decades," Amanda joked. She saw no humor in her father's eyes as he stared back at her from the doorway.

In that moment Amanda wished she had brought the backpack up the steps with her. She hadn't dared to after her father had questioned her about carrying it out to the car. She had told him another half-truth, saying that she just didn't feel prepared without it anymore. She had even forced a smile and quipped, "Be ready..." But he had only frowned in response as if annoyed.

Inside there was a large red and blue "grand opening" banner displayed above the glass counter top. The cash register was no doubt an antique itself. It looked as though it was made of brass, and it had round black and white buttons protruding from its front. Beside it, a silver bell was labeled "Ring for service."

Amanda peered into the display case, which was filled with daggers and figurines. Everything inside sparkled, as if each item had been meticulously cleaned and polished, despite the fact that the floor had a layer of dust on it that left a shoeprint wherever she stepped.

Single light bulbs hung from the rafters, swaying back and forth, casting a light glow around the room. Amanda scanned shelves crammed with books in many different languages. A chest half pushed under one of the shelves caught her eye, and she pulled it out to look at the designs carved into it. She had hoped they would be familiar to her, but the more she studied them, the more they lost all resemblance to the ones she had seen on the dagger image and Erol's prison. Amanda nearly jumped out of her shoes when her father rang the bell.

The clerk appeared from behind a dusty tapestry that was hanging above a doorway into a back area. She watched as the man curled his fingers around the end of his long beard as her father described something to him. Amanda strained her ears, but it was no use, she couldn't make out their soft murmurs. She moved deliberately toward them, pretending to be interested in a gaudy-looking vase a few feet closer. She reached for the vase, but just as she had gotten close enough to hear, they stopped talking.

The clerk moved to unlock a glass case. Tony turned toward her so quickly that she almost dropped the vase in surprise. The seller, Oolas, she assumed, paused momentarily, eyeing her with distrust before resuming his task. Amanda blinked a few times. *I have never seen such odd gray eyes.* She turned and set the vase back on the shelf.

"Did you find anything interesting, Mandy?" Amanda rolled her eyes at the nickname. "Not really," she lied. Everything in here was interesting; she just couldn't focus on any of it. The clerk slid her father a package wrapped in paper and tied with a string. She thought she saw him wink at her father as he picked it up, but the flickering lights must have been playing tricks on her eyes.

Amanda was relieved to be out of the store and on her way back home. She laid her head on the car door and closed her eyes as her father drove. Sick of the awkward silence between them, she pretended to be asleep.

Her head bounced slightly off the glass, and Amanda opened her eyes and sat up as she felt the car swerve and stop, causing her body to jerk forward.

She looked around, expecting to see another car or an animal motionless in the road nearby, but the street appeared to be empty besides their own vehicle.

"Are you okay?" she blurted, assessing her father's condition. He looked at her with the same strange smile from the morning curled onto his lips.

"Could you tell me about her?" He breathed out smoothly, as if stopping dead in the street and having a chat was the most normal thing in the world.

"What?" Amanda turned in her seat to get a better look at her father. "What are you doing? Did we almost hit something?"

Tony rested his hands in his lap. "I thought we could talk."

"Here? In the middle of the street? Dad, what is wrong with you?"

Tony frowned and looked down at his hands. "Just later, okay, we will talk." He closed his eyes and took a deep breath.

Amanda couldn't bring herself to look away. "Dad, do you need to go to the hospital or something?"

"No," he whispered, barely loud enough for her to hear. He squinted his eyes tighter, and she could see lines form on his brow. He breathed in deeply and again opened his eyes, looking around wildly.

"Dad?"

Tony rubbed at his eyes. "Must have dozed off for a second. I'm, I'm sorry if I scared you."

"Dad, what is going on?"

"Nothing, nothing," he murmured, looking out at the road. "I just haven't been sleeping well. Let's get home." Amanda could see his hands tremble as he returned them to the steering wheel. She didn't dare take her eyes off him for the rest of the ride home.

8

Amanda decided to surprise her father by making dinner. She cut and rinsed vegetables for salad, boiled water for pasta, and simmered sauce on the stove. Her father had not left his study since they had returned, and Amanda felt a little pang of guilt for all the silence between them.

She knocked on the door. "Dinner in ten, Dad." She received no reply but went about setting the table and straining the noodles. Amanda was no chef, but her father was generally not too picky. She walked back to the study door when everything was ready. "Dad?" she asked as she knocked again and pushed the door open.

He sat at his desk, studying something in his hand. Amanda stepped into the room. The brown paper and string from the package he had brought home were now empty and thrown across the floor. Curious, Amanda took a step closer to see what he had purchased.

Tony dropped the thing on the desk and stood suddenly, as if Amanda had startled him awake. He hurried out the door, pushing past her.

Amanda glanced at the object on the desk; unease blossomed within her. It was the dagger from the photo, she was sure. She had seen the expression on Erol's face when he glimpsed pictures of the dagger. He had been afraid, no, he had been terrified,

Amanda needed to know why. Her stomach felt like lead as she left the room and shut the door behind her.

Knowing she couldn't just race upstairs with her backpack, she tried to seem interested in the dinner she had prepared.

"How did it turn out?" she asked as she took the seat across from her father.

He twisted the cap from a bottle of painkillers and swallowed them without the aid of liquid. "Fine." He grunted as he reached up to massage his temples.

"Dad, are you sure you shouldn't see a doctor?" she asked as she twirled noodles around her fork. She had lost her appetite. She had been trying to think of a good reason to go outside and summon Erol. She didn't want to take a chance at her father overhearing them.

He grimaced as he looked at his plate. "Sorry." He pushed the dish away. "I don't think I can eat." He stared down at the table. "These headaches... it feels like something is clawing at my brain."

Amanda stood, lifting his untouched plate "It's okay, I will clean everything up." She placed her hand on his shoulder and felt him flinch at her touch. She backed away. "Maybe you should go rest."

Tony stood and made his way out of the room as Amanda dumped the uneaten food into the trash. As Amanda lifted the half full plastic trash bag from the garbage, Tony reappeared from around the corner, his eyes wide. He grunted and slurred as his lip drooped slightly.

"Am, Amanda, could you tell me the story of how we met."

Amanda loosened her grip on the bag. "What are you talking about?"

"Your mom and me." This fell out his mouth more naturally.

Amanda looked him up and down, unsure how to respond to the strange question.

"Dad, are you sure you're okay? Maybe I should I call an ambulance?"

Tony looked down at his feet and Amanda saw a bit a drool slide from the corner of his mouth. "That's it, go up to bed. I'm calling the doctor as soon as I'm done with this." Amanda gestured toward the garbage.

"Bed?"

"Go." Amanda pointed toward the stairs and watched as he ascended.

She removed the garbage bag to carry it out and snatched her backpack up on her way to the door. Outside, she was misted by light rain as she dropped the garbage into its can and walked around the side of the house, whispering to Erol.

Erol had a solemn expression on his face as he appeared. *He already knows the dagger is here.* "You need to tell me why you're afraid of that thing."

He flung his hands up in the air. "It's dangerous, that's all that you need to know." He paced back and forth in front of Amanda as she tried to reason with him.

"There's something wrong with my father. Does it have anything to do with the dagger?" Erol looked away, and Amanda placed her hands on her hips. "Why was he looking for that thing anyway? Erol, I need to know. There is something you're not telling me!" she managed as she heard the front door bang against the side of the house as if it had been flung wide open, interrupting her.

"Amanda," her father yelled. The urgency in his voice caused her to rush back around the side of the house to the door. "There you are," he said as he backed up to let her in. Amanda felt the light pressure of Erol's hand on her back; she didn't have to turn around to know he was not visible. He was just letting her know he was still there.

Amanda started to explain that she had heard a strange noise behind the house and had gone to investigate. The vacant look in her father's eyes sent a shiver down her spine. As Amanda spoke the lie, he brought his hand out from behind his back. Frightened by the sight of the dagger in his hand, she backed away, just as he turned toward her. Tony lunged at her, his mouth formed into a maniacal grin, his eyebrows arched menacingly as he started to approach her again.

Amanda's heart pounded as she turned to run away from the madman. She only managed a few feet before she felt arms grab her from behind, wrapping around her waist.

She screamed and flailed, struggling to be released from the strong grip. Amanda couldn't believe what was happening. Her own father was trying to stab her.

"Stop," Erol yelled into her ear. Confusion assailed her mind. *Was Erol trying to help him or me?*

"Let me go," she screamed as he pulled at her waist again, tightening his grip. She could hear her father laughing loudly as the room seemed to crumble away and she was encircled by blinding light.

Amanda had been here before. "You're safe," a whisper close to her ear reassured her. She could still feel Erol's arm tightly wrapped around her. His form seemed solid, yet she could see only the outline. He was transparent. "Where are we?" she asked as her eyes started to adjust to the bright light. "I brought you to a different plane," he explained. "We must go back; you cannot survive here long."

"Is this your home?" she probed.

"No," he responded. "It is not easy for a human to go to the plane of the jinn."

"Why did my father attack me?" She knew that he had some kind of idea what was going on. "My father is not some psycho," Amanda said, more to herself than him.

"I don't think it was your father that attacked you, Amanda, but we must go back now."

They reappeared on a street that Amanda recognized; they were a few blocks from her home. The rain had stopped, and the sun was shining down on them. *It seems like we were only gone for a few minutes, but how long was it?*

Erol must have sensed the question on her lips. "Time works differently in that plane," he offered. "It's one of the reasons you cannot be there long."

They walked toward her house in silence. Amanda stopped short as her home came into view. Yellow caution tape stretched around the yard, blocking anyone from entering. The odor of smoke lingered in the air. A few people stood at the edge of the tape, staring at the charred remains of her once normal-looking home.

A female reporter stood in front of a camera aimed toward the burned rubble. "The home was already completely engulfed in flames when the firefighters arrived last night after receiving a call from a neighbor. Firefighters say it is still unclear if it was arson, pending further investigation. What is thought to be the homeowner, Dr. Tony Garrett's remains were pulled from the inferno by rescue workers."

Amanda moved to run toward the house, but Erol clasped her arm firmly, stopping her.

"They are still searching the debris to determine if his fifteen-year-old daughter, Amanda Garrett, was home at the time of the fire. Neighbors reported seeing her around the property early in the evening."

Amanda wanted to run to the woman. Her face was wet with tears; her father was her only family. Her hands shook as Erol pulled her back, trying to move her away from the scene. "It's not safe here," he urged. But Amanda couldn't take her eyes off the house. She felt so alone as she stared up at its skeleton.

The house let out a sudden groan, and then a cracking noise could be heard as several rescue workers scrambled out the front door. The glass in the few remaining windows shattered as the house folded in on itself. People screamed and rushed away to safety on the other side of the street. Finally breaking the trance, Amanda turned to Erol and let him pull her away.

She didn't know how long he led her that way. He didn't stop until they were far from all the houses and noise. She collapsed in the grass, still in a stupor. Erol sat down beside her, taking her hand gently in his. Amanda laid her head on his shoulder, the tears still streaming steadily down her cheeks. They stayed that way unmoving until she stopped shaking and the tears seemed to slow.

Erol took her chin in his hand. "Amanda," he said, trying to see if she would respond now. Amanda blinked the last of the tears away as he looked into her eyes. "I'm sorry," he said, releasing her chin and her gaze.

He looked at the ground and picked at the grass beside him. "An ifrit," he spat out. Not understanding, Amanda looked at him questioningly. "I said it wasn't your father who attacked you. He was possessed by an ifrit." He looked back up at her as if he had more to say but remained quiet for a moment. "We need to go somewhere farther away. You are not safe."

"But why?" she muttered. "Why is this happening, Erol?" She grabbed his arm but turned her face away from him, guessing the answer before he had a chance to explain.

"You sound scared, Amanda. Good, you should be." He tore his arm from her grasp. "You must realize there are creatures that would use me for things that you couldn't even begin to imagine. And the only way for them to have me now is to take me from you forcefully. I am bound to you."

"And if I give you to them?"

He looked away from her gaze. "You can't. As I have already explained to you."

"Bring my father back then," she demanded.

"I can't, Amanda." He let out a sigh "You cannot bring people back from the dead, at least not how you're asking."

"You have taken everything from me," she yelled, jumping to her feet.

"Please, Amanda," he begged. "We couldn't have stopped it." Amanda could see hurt in his eyes. She was glad he had to feel some of her pain. She thought about letting the backpack fall to the ground and simply walking away. *What would happen?* She didn't know. But she didn't think it would help the pain she was already feeling. "Where do we go?" she asked.

"Nowhere will be safe for long. Somebody is controlling the ifrit," Erol said weakly. "We need to know who or what we are up against. I have an idea, but I am not sure."

"Is there a way to free you?" Amanda asked.

"Death," he said coldly, looking down at his feet.

9

Amanda walked on, following Erol, the events still swirling in her head. She wrung her hands nervously as they boarded a bus, not caring where Erol was leading her. She watched out the window in her trance-like state, blind to her surroundings as the scenery sped by until the driver announced the last stop, end of the line. *End of the line.* Even then Erol had to pull her from the seat to get her to exit the bus.

Amanda remained in her stupor as she stood on the steps outside of a hotel, watching Erol through a set of wide glass doors as he negotiated with a tall redhead at the concierge desk. She saw no money exchange hands, yet a rectangular plastic key card was produced from behind the desk, allowing them access to a room.

The springs squeaked as Amanda lay on the bed, staring up at the ceiling, wishing her simple plastic stars were there instead of smeared red marks that she had no doubt were the remains of squashed bugs. She wanted to be alone, but Erol sat down on the edge of the bed beside her.

She tried to pay attention as he finally broke the silence.

He began to tell her stories he had learned from his childhood. Amanda half listened, knowing she was probably missing important information, but she felt distant, numb inside and out.

"An ifrit," he said, finally jarring her back to reality, "is a jinni, like me. But one that has chosen a path of evil in one way or another." Amanda tried to concentrate on the sound of his voice. "All jinn have free will, like humans, unless it is taken from them." From the way he described the place he was from and his family, it seemed he had at one point lived a life not unlike her own. "A jinni will never turn down a challenge or a chance to show off." He smirked, trying to break her silence.

Amanda thought about the things he had said; it seemed to her that they were a mischievous but peaceful bunch. *Of course, there are exceptions in every society, aren't there. Otherwise, there would be no reason to punish anyone.* He had said that his entrapment was a punishment. Amanda wondered to herself why but thought he would tell her when he trusted her. *Should I trust him?*

Amanda just wanted to be alone. She closed her eyes and tried to clear her mind of all thought, hoping that Erol would assume she had drifted off to sleep. It must have worked, because the murmur of his voice soon faded from her ears. She glanced beside her, still trying to hold her mind at bay; he was no longer sitting where she could see him.

She sat up and took in her surroundings for the first time since they had arrived. Her last few days had been anything but average, so the sight of what seemed like a perfectly normal room was not at all what she had expected.

There was a lamp and a writing desk, even an old television with rabbit ears resting on a small table in front of the double bed. She hadn't seen a big, bulky TV like that in ages. There were no windows in the room for her to gauge the time of day. She spotted a rectangular clock, the red numbers flashing 12:00 repeatedly.

Her backpack rested propped up by the door to the bathroom. She eyed it as she stood; without further thought she walked out the door, leaving her possessions behind.

She wanted space; she needed to get away from Erol for a little while.

She knew he would have tried to talk her out of it if she had told him that she wanted to be alone. Amanda walked around the block three times before she felt better. She couldn't place the sole blame of what had occurred on Erol; after all, he was in just as much danger as she was, *isn't he?*

Each time she passed the little cafe on the corner, she breathed in the aroma of fresh ground coffee all around her. She longed to sit and have a cup. She was not particularly fond of coffee, but the smell reminded her of her own house in the morning. She craved the normalcy of it, the idea of sitting and sipping as hot steam rose from the warm cup.

A few empty chairs were scattered around the area outside. Three round wooden tables with brown umbrellas sticking out of their centers tempted her at each pass.

As she rounded the corner for the fourth time, she paused and her heart skipped a beat as she took in the man now seated in one of the chairs, a newspaper spread out in front of him.

Suddenly thinking only of her father, she starred in the man's direction as he lowered the paper.

The man seemed to be the same age as her father, but that's where the resemblance ended. His eyes looked almost gray. *Weird coincidence,* she thought, remembering Oolas and the way his eyes had seemed to be an oddly similar shade. *How well did I really see him in the dim lighting?* Goosebumps prickled on her arms. *No, you're being crazy again.* His hair was speckled with the same shade of gray. *He really does look familiar, though,* Amanda thought as she tried to place where else she could have seen him.

He motioned toward her like they were old friends.

Amanda walked over to apologize for staring. "I'm sorry, I thought you were someone else."

He laughed at that. "I thought the same, young lady."

Amanda apologized again. "I didn't mean to stare."

"You look lost. We have all been there before. Come sit and have a cup of coffee with me." His eyes seemed to dance as he pleaded. Amanda pulled the chair out and sat before she even realized what she was doing. *Maybe I don't want to be alone after all.*

"Jacob," he said, holding out his hand.

"Amanda," she introduced herself, not wanting to offend him further. Amanda accepted his hand but fought not to pull back as his cold skin touched hers, sending chills through her arm.

He set a cup of hot coffee in front of her, and she pressed her now-cold hand into the hot ceramic mug, trying to chase away the chill. *Were there two cups all along?* she wondered as he sipped from the mug. *Was I staring so hard, I missed the waitress?* Even though his eyes returned to the paper, she felt like he was watching her.

Amanda gulped the coffee down, burning her throat. *What am I doing? This guy could be a serial killer.* She glanced around uneasily; there was still not another soul in sight. "I'm sorry, I shouldn't have sat down; I have somewhere I need to go." She stood up and pushed the chair in toward the table.

"Thank you for the coffee," she blurted as she backed up a few steps. The need to get away was almost painful. Something wasn't right. Something was urging her back to Erol. Pulling her.

"Stay," the man said, folding the paper in front of him. He pressed his fingers to his lips and whispered something else she couldn't quite hear. Amanda's legs stopped working. She pleaded with her body to shift, but it was no use. Her heart started racing as the man stood and walked around her.

He mumbled, "Quiet." She could feel his eyes on her, cold and metallic, looking her up and down. Amanda opened her mouth to scream, but no sound would come out.

"Hmmm." He tapped his chin." You are much weaker than I thought you would be." This had to be the man they were trying to avoid. *Dammit.* She cursed herself for being so stupid.

"Walk to that white van over there," he said, pointing. Amanda's legs obeyed, and she strolled in the direction he indicated. She came to an abrupt stop beside the vehicle. She tried to tell her body to run, but it was no use.

Jacob bound her hands together with rope and shoved her into the vehicle. The door made a loud bang as it slid shut, causing Amanda to wince.

She tested her arms and legs by lifting them a few inches above the floor, satisfied that she could once again command her own body. She pushed herself up onto her knees. The tight rope cut into her skin as she tried to wiggle her hands loose. She heard the loud roar of the engine. The van wrenched forward violently, causing her to fall backward; there was a thud as her head collided with the metal floor, and pain radiated in her skull from the impact. Amanda closed her eyes and groaned. She only had time for one thought to form before everything went black.

10

The thought was still reverberating in her head when she finally woke; the air felt damp.

The floor was hard and cold. For a moment she thought it had all been a dream. She was still in the woods alone, trapped underground, surrounded by unending darkness. But this place was different. Amanda could feel small ruts pressing into her skin like cut stone, and she could hear dripping somewhere nearby.

Did he drug me? she wondered as she pulled herself up and tried to stand, her hands still bound together by the rope. *No, it was a spell, something he muttered.* It took her a moment to get her feet under her. She carefully turned in a circle.

Amanda was in an empty room surrounded by ancient stone walls. They rose up on all sides. She couldn't make out the outline of a single door or window. In the gloom, everything appeared to be a different shade of gray.

"Hello?" she whispered into the unlit room. She waited for a moment. The only noise was the sound of water dripping somewhere nearby. She called louder this time. "Hello?"

"Lo," echoed back.

A few sudden bright white sparks in the distance caught her attention. She turned toward the odd light that appeared to be coming through a stacked layer in the stone wall.

She watched as the sparks grew into a small orange flame that seemed to be getting closer. The flame turned red and then blue as it burned and grew, lighting up the room. Her heart pounded as the nearing fire started morphing into something else, slowly taking on the shape of a person. As it got closer, she could feel the heat on her skin, at first warm and inviting and then burning just up to the point where she could barely stand it. Beads of sweat bloomed on her forehead. Amanda looked around the room again, but even in the newly glowing light, it didn't appear there was any way out of the fire monster's reach.

This had to be the evil jinn that Erol had told her about, the thing that had taken her father from her. She looked at the demon, refusing to cower, as thoughts and memories of her father assailed her. He would never again scold her, or laugh with her, or tell her about her mother. She felt tears start to pool in her eyes; she had no home to go back to. Still, she refused to look away from the unmoving green eyes.

The creature stared back, unblinking. Amanda's head started to throb. Slowly she lifted one leg and bent forward, and reaching with her bound hands, she wobbled slightly as she worked her shoe from her foot. With both feet back on the floor, she let out a bloodcurdling scream and did her best to fling her shoe at the jinn.

A large wave of gray smoke rolled toward Amanda, surrounding her, choking her. She doubled over in a coughing fit as her lungs fought for clean air. When the smoke cleared and Amanda was able to breathe again, the fire monster was gone.

Amanda sank to the stone floor and closed her eyes. *This can't be happening.*

Amanda felt a light tickle on her cheek; she brushed it away with her hand. The tickle moved through it and stayed there, causing it to tingle in an unusual way. She forced her puffy eyes open. The room was filled with a soft blue glow.

Touching her hand was a small blue wispy ball. She jerked her hand back, pulling it the rest of the way through the creature. The tingling stopped, and the ball rose upward toward the ceiling. Following it with her eyes, she could see them hovering there, dozens of fist-sized balls of blue light.

She did not speak for fear of scaring them off.

Silently, she wondered how they had come to be in this desolate place with her as they moved and spun around one another. Her legs felt wobbly as she stood. She leaned against the wall to steady herself. Her hand grew wet from the moisture penetrating the stones.

Amanda's tongue felt bumpy and swollen; she realized how dry her mouth was. She followed the wall with her hand as she moved toward the dripping she still heard.

There was a crack in the uppermost part of the wall that ran about two feet along the ceiling. The water was slowly trickling in. Amanda cupped her bound hands under it and waited for her palms to fill.

She managed to suck most of it up, spilling only a little in the process. She had expected the water to be contaminated in some way. It tasted normal, almost fresh. She repeated this maneuver several times until her stomach let out a fierce growl.

Amanda lowered herself back to the floor. Shards of stone from the crumbling, cracked wall dug into her knees as she sifted through the pieces, trying to find the sharpest rock she could. It took several tries before she was able to firmly grasp one with her fingers. Maybe there was still room for hope. She had to try. She twisted her wrists around awkwardly, trying to make the edge of the stone reach the rope binding. She sawed at it in slow, careful motions.

The muffled sound of voices came from the other side of the wall; she stood slowly, careful to keep a tight grip on the small, sharp stone. She scooted away from her place by the wall and the blue glow of the wisps vanished just as the stones began to shift and the outline of a door began to appear.

Her eyes did not have time to adjust as once again the room was filled with light. But instead of the low glow from the wisps, a much harsher, brighter light brought moisture to Amanda's confused eyes. It took them a moment to regain focus.

Two men came through the misshapen door that had emerged. No, that was wrong. One was in the shape of a man but looked like a giant piece of coal that had been plucked and carved directly from a hot fire. You could see sparks of orange and blue in the cracks and crevasses of his blackened flesh. The creature looked at her with his green eyes, and Amanda realized it was the same monster that had ignited in the room before.

She looked into the other man's face and recognized the pale gray eyes beaming at her and the mess of speckled gray hair.

Amanda thought of the stone, and trying to keep eye contact with the man and his attention from her hands, she asked, "What do you want with me?" as she attempted to cup it into her palm. It seemed like a simple question, since Amanda thought she had already knew the answer; he wanted Erol, and even more so, he wanted her dead.

A cruel smile spread across his lips. "I want you to help me." His voice echoed through the room as she felt a hard, stinging slap across her face, making her already watery eyes flood. She was sure if she could look in a mirror there would have been a perfect imprint of his hand there.

"There is no escape for you," he growled. He forcefully cupped Amanda's chin so that she could not look away. He grabbed her hand and forced it open, then blew onto the stone. Amanda watched it crumble into dust. As he released her face, she recoiled. "The fun is just starting, Amanda. Such an enjoyable game we played. I do so love acting."

"You are the man from the antique shop, aren't you?" She spat. *I'm not crazy.*

"Yes, well, Someone else wasn't doing a very good job." He made a fast motion toward the ifrit. "Causing you to ask all sorts of questions. Forcing me to change tactics."

Amanda envisioned the stretcher being carried from her house as it burned. She felt a tear roll down her cheek, and she rubbed her bound hands against her face to wipe it away. *He won't see me cry.* "How do you want me to help you?" Her voice quivered.

"I seek a talisman. A relic of sorts. A ring." His eyes shifted to the ifrit then back to Amanda. "A legendary ring that is said to have the power to control all jinn. You will find it for me."

Amanda looked at the ifrit that stood there watching, waiting for orders. "But you already have a jinni in your control."

"One is not enough. I need to control all of their race for what I'm planning." Jacob reached out toward Amanda, and she backed away, shaking her head.

"I'm not going to help you."

"No?" His manic grin widened. "Well, let's see if I can help you then." The man who had called himself Jacob laughed as his hand went to Amanda's shoulder, pressing her down forcefully onto her knees. "Don't move."

Amanda bit into her lip to keep herself from screaming out as he produced a short, thin knife.

She looked up at the ifrit, pleading with her eyes, but just as their gaze met he turned away from her, an unreadable expression on his face.

Jacob started to speak a strange language as he lifted the dagger steadily, moving it toward the surface of her skin.

Amanda tried to move away but was unable to convince her arms and legs to work. She felt her muscles tighten in anticipation of the pain she knew was coming.

Jacob began to mumble the incantation faster as the dagger dragged across her flesh, slicing just beneath the skin on her back shoulder blade.

She bit down harder then, and her mouth filled with the taste of iron. Searing, fiery bursts pulsated around the wound as he lifted the dagger away, just to bring it back down again onto a new piece of flesh.

Unable to bear the torture, Amanda let out a sharp scream and found herself unable to stop until her throat grew raw and she no longer had the ability to produce more than a grunt. By then he had lifted the knife and brought it back down onto her flesh seven times, carving into the thin skin, from right to left along her back shoulders.

Amanda went quiet, just panting, her face frozen in a grimace, consumed by the pain. Her brain was emitting nothing except a nonproductive fuzz.

"You will help me one way or another." His hold on her released, and she fell forward, exhausted, onto the palms of her hands. "And you can stay down here until you appreciate me a little more, I think."

Amanda could barely register the grinding of the stones shifting back into their original formation as the door disappeared, along with her tormentors.

She lay on the ground, her skin pale and clammy, her teeth gritted, her vision blotched with violent colors that moved around without a pattern. Amanda closed her eyes and sucked herself into a deeper place to cope.

Amanda didn't know how long she lay there, thinking about death and the peace it could bring her. The situation seemed hopeless, even if she survived this. She could feel blood oozing from the wounds across her back.

The side of her face felt swollen as she touched it with her bound hands. Amanda had nothing to look forward to, even if she made it out of here alive. She couldn't return to the home she had always known; she would never again have a normal life.

She was filled with emptiness; a dark despair settled over her. Every way forward was blocked at all points. The notion of hope had become meaningless, the idea of it a cruel joke. She lay on the stone floor feeling sorry for herself.

This time sleep took her away. A warm breeze blew past her as she stood in the field. Her heart quickened; there in the distance, she could just make out Erol's shape coming toward her. She tested her legs, and they moved. Amanda ran toward him as fast as she could, but for each step she took forward, he seemed to be moving an equal step away.

Amanda stopped and listened to the whisper of the wind, never taking her eyes from the figure of Erol. It was his voice that carried to her with each new gust. She had to strain to understand the words. He was telling her something she needed to hear.

"Things work differently in dreams, Amanda. They are not always safe."

"Is this a real place?"

He smiled in the distance. "As real as any other place you have been." Amanda opened her mouth to say more, to tell him she had been here before, but he raised his arm and opened his hand, motioning her to stop.

"I do not have much time, and if the Arcane sorcerer finds out that I visited you here, he will make sure it doesn't happen again." Erol's gaze shifted from Amanda's eyes to her torn shirt. He spoke more softly. "What has he done to you?" His lips were pressed together in a thin line. "He won't get away with this." Erol grimaced at the sight of the wounds. "I know you are lonely and afraid. They will only keep me from you until you obey his demands." He was closer now. Almost close enough to touch, although he did not appear to have been moving as he spoke. "What did he ask you to do?"

"He wants us to help him find something, a ring."

Erol's brow furrowed, and he looked around as if searching for something or someone. When his eyes rested back on Amanda, he added, "Then that's what we will appear to do."

Erol reached out to her, and Amanda copied the gesture. Their hands met for just one moment as his form disintegrated before her eyes. She remained there with her arm outstretched, expecting to wake immediately. She blinked a few times and dropped her arm, studying the field that was once again before her.

Amanda tried to walk to one of the wildflowers she had admired before. But as she stepped forward, they too seemed to move back. She thought of what Erol had said about things working differently and how he had not appeared to be walking when he had gotten closer. Staying still, she looked at the flower and concentrated on it. Sure, enough the view seemed to shift in her direction, slowly pulling the field and flower toward her.

Amanda's excitement at finally seeing one up close was short-lived. As she reached out to feel the large, soft petals, they wilted under her fingers. She tried again, and again the next flower wilted at her touch. Perplexed, she thought of the golden apples that had fallen from the tree that now seemed miles away from her. Amanda's stomach rumbled as the tree came nearer. She scooped one up; it felt solid in her hand. She brought it to her lips and tasted. Her mouth was filled with ash as that too crumbled in her grasp.

Amanda awoke to the light of the mysterious wisps. One hovered near her face. There was something inside it. It was another sharp stone. Still afraid she would scare it off with the sound of her voice, she just nodded up and down as if to say yes. It moved closer to her, and she felt a strange tingling sensation as it touched her hand and released the stone into it. She went to work at the rope once again. Her bloody muscles quivered with each movement.

Amanda's wrists were raw from the friction, and she was sure they were bruising. But she kept at it until she finally felt the rope loosen and fall away. More of the wisps had returned. The room glowed brighter with their light. They helped refresh that hopeful feeling within her. Her mouth was hot and dry, and her throat ached. She needed a drink of something. The pain radiating from her shoulders intensified with each dragging step as she made her way back to the cracked area of the wall.

Amanda let some of the water trickle onto her face and onto her brutalized shoulders. It stung her sore cheek, and as it dripped down her back, she gasped as fresh, sharp pain reverberated from the wounds. She reached around, fingering one of the shapes with the lightest touch possible.

It was much easier to drink the water with her hands free. Her broken body felt sore and tired, and her stomach, although sloshing with water, felt hollow.

Amanda thought about how it would be to die here, no one even aware that you were missing. *No one is looking for you.* She tried to force the thoughts from her head, but in the gloom of her prison, it was impossible to keep them at bay.

She watched as a larger wisp came toward her. The wisp was completely engulfing something that shimmered.

Amanda let it drop into her outstretched hand. It was an apple with golden skin, like the one she had seen in her dream with Erol. She wondered if it too would crumble. Her mouth started to water, and her belly let out a fearsome growl. She bit into it, and it broke between her teeth with a soft crunch.

A sudden numbness caused her to stop chewing; it started in her mouth and radiated outward around her face and down her back. Amanda swallowed and took another bite, reaching for her shoulder with her free hand. The cuts remained, but the pain was gone, even if the effect was only temporary; Amanda couldn't help herself this time as she let a thank-you escape from her lips.

Just as she had feared, the wisps made themselves scarce. The room was once again gloomy and dark. Amanda scolded herself. *Why did I do that? Why did I scare them away?* She held out hope that they would return as she lowered herself back onto the cold stone floor.

She needed something to do, something to keep her mind busy while she waited for the Arcane sorcerer to return. She had tried calling to Jacob, but if he or the ifrit heard, they did nothing about it.

When the wisps finally did come back, they appeared just a few at a time. Amanda was thankful for their glow, even if they stayed at a distance. She was comforted by them. She felt like they were somehow keeping watch. She did not dare try to speak again for fear she would be left without their light.

Amanda found that she could etch pictures on the stone walls with a sharp rock. She had never thought of herself as much of an artist; she had always been more interested in outdoor activities and sports, but there was nothing else for her to do.

With no particular image in mind, she began to doodle on one of walls. A few circles here, a line or two there. She was just passing the time. Soon strange designs began to emerge, and Amanda couldn't help but wonder if she had harbored some natural talent for drawing all along.

It seemed like days had passed since the sorcerer had last appeared by the time she had covered the reachable part of the first wall. She tried to calculate how many times her stomach had growled until the wisps brought her fruit, quieting it. And how many times sleep had overtaken her, but she had no real way of keeping track.

Erol had never returned to her in her dreams. She knew that the sorcerer had done something to prevent him from finding her there. Jacob seemed to be enjoying her torment; she had seen it in his eyes the day he inflicted the scars into her back. Each time she had screamed, he only grinned wider.

She took a step back from the wall to get a better view of her work. The countless episodes of scribbling had somehow joined and converged, creating an odd display.

At the center was the tree from the woods, complete with barren, crooked branches and strange shapes drawn on the bark. Some type of carrion birds circled the figure of a girl, their talons at the ready. Above the scene a menacing face stared back at her, with an unnaturally wide smile. Amidst the pictures words were written in a large and bold hand: YOU'RE RUNNING OUT OF TIME.

Amanda's stomach turned. She tried to close her eyes and think of the hot sun on her face instead of the unsettling artwork. She could feel her despair rooting itself deep inside. She stopped taking water from the broken wall, even when her lips felt dry and cracked. The wisps tried to bring her more fruit, but she refused it. Soon their light faded altogether, as if they too realized her cause was hopeless and she was doomed. They seemed to have given up on her.

As the door reappeared, Amanda could make out just the outline of light around it. She didn't have the energy to crawl to it. She didn't think it would be necessary anyway. Surely if the door was back, so was the sorcerer. *It could be the end of me, a blissful end.* Amanda was ready for it. There was absolutely nothing left for her here. No parents, no home, not even Erol. She smiled and welcomed the release he would give her.

11

Jacob rubbed his hands together; he seemed to be encouraged by the sight of Amanda's despair. *Death won't be enough for him. He wants me to suffer for eternity. Either in his dungeon or by his side.*

"You're a monster," Amanda managed.

"No, I am a visionary. I'm going to help you unlock what's inside of you," he replied, his eyes dancing with excitement. "I don't care what you think of me, as long as you obey. I acknowledge that I have less than desirable methods, but they do work, eventually." He circled her body on the floor. Stopping in front of the eerie images on the wall, he turned and smiled at her, as if pleased with what he saw, waiting for her to speak again.

Amanda stood, wobbling on her feet. The fruits the wisps had been bringing her were no longer heaped by her side but had been laid out before the opposite wall in the shape of letters. MUST SURVI was as far as she got before the sorcerer kicked at the fruits, sending them skittering around the floor.

Amanda realized with sudden clarity that things wouldn't be simple. *This is all still some kind of game.* She knew he wasn't about to pretend to be anything other than what he was, pure evil. She couldn't let Erol be controlled by this beast of a man. She would find a way to be Erol's heroine. Still, Amanda felt like she was being weak. How would she be able to help Erol if she couldn't help herself? How much longer before she would start having delusions and become just as mad as the sorcerer seemed?

"Well, Amanda?"

Amanda nodded in response; she wouldn't last much longer down here alone, with nothing but her thoughts to keep her company.

Jacob steadied her with both arms as she stumbled through the narrow passageway, falling back to her knees. He grunted and hefted her body over his shoulder. His footsteps echoed as he carried her up several flights of dark steps made of twisted rock.

He placed her on a bed in a room, shutting the door behind him. Amanda heard the click of a key turn in the lock as she forced herself to sit up. Next to her on a small table was a glass of water and a plate of small sandwiches.

She sipped the glass slowly at first, but it didn't take her long to empty it completely. She set it back down on the table and nibbled a sandwich. She almost spat the sandwich back out as she watched the glass refill with water. *Nothing should surprise me anymore,* she thought as she sipped again from the glass. She could feel her strength returning.

Amanda felt better, although guilt was gnawing at her as her sensibilities came back. She wondered what exactly she had agreed to and where they could be keeping Erol.

The sound of water rushing was constant and seemed to be everywhere at once. There was a slit in the stone wall, a skinny window of sorts. Amanda walked to the opening and peered out. Water seemed to cascade down around her stone tower from above, like a continuous rain storm. Patches of bright green moss clung to the rocks. The running water distorted the view beyond; she thought she could make out the glass-like shimmer of a pond and a field in the distance. There was no sign of life besides the vegetation.

Is this all real or an illusion? Amanda reached out to feel the icy cold spray on her skin. It felt real enough; she wished she could squeeze her whole head out into the clean, fresh air. She pressed her face hard against the opening and breathed in deeply, then pulled back.

Standing here isn't going to help anything. There would be no knight in shining armor rushing toward her tower or men in orange vests to come to her rescue. She would have to play along until an opportunity presented itself, or she could make one.

Amanda scanned the room. Apart from the bed and small table, the only other furniture was a tall wooden wardrobe. She pulled it open, jumping slightly as she was met by her own disheveled reflection in one of the doors. There was an iron basin on one of the shelves, and Amanda filled it from the cup and attempted to clean herself up.

Several pieces of clothing hung on one side of the closet, all black. Amanda chose the items she felt would cover her now even slimmer body in the most tasteful way. Her cheeks burned as she studied the form-fitting outfit and knee-length boots that now clung to her skin. The boots were more comfortable than Amanda had expected, and she tied her hair back out of her face, revealing the scars on her shoulder blades.

They looked like angry carvings; the raised lines were still bright red and puffy.

Amanda closed the doors and turned to see the evil jinn materializing before her. As he solidified into the strange charcoal form she had seen before, she couldn't help letting curiosity get the better of her, and she reached out. His skin was not hard like stone, nor as soft as flesh. It felt coarse and hot against her fingertips. He hissed and drew back at her touch.

Amanda crossed her arms over her chest and waited for him to speak, looking down at her feet, sorry she had touched him.

"I am to take you downstairs." The jinn's voice caused the hairs on the back of her neck to stand up. She had never heard him speak before; his voice was deep and hollow.

Amanda looked up into his eyes as she moved to follow. She thought she could see pain and confusion. Had her touch hurt him somehow? It hadn't seemed to hurt Erol, and weren't they after all in some way the same type of being?

"What's your name…" she started to ask, but he turned toward her, stopping her. Amanda took a step back, afraid she had been mistaken. That what she had seen in his eyes had actually been anger.

"You have no power over me, and I do not intend to give you any." He turned away and continued to lead her down the passageway and into a hall.

"When can I see Erol?" she asked, just as he stopped in front of a sturdy wooden door. The jinn didn't respond as he pulled the looping metal handle, dragging the door open.

"Wait here." He gestured into a room that seemed to be filled with dancing candlelight. Every inch of the walls was covered by shelves that overflowed with books. A large wooden desk and matching solid chair sat in the center.

As he dispersed into the air. Amanda felt a tightening around her ankle. She reached down and tugged at the shackle that had appeared from nowhere. The cold, hard metal bit into her leg just enough to cause discomfort.

Amanda guessed trust from Jacob didn't come easily. But where did he expect her to run to? She glanced around the library again, eyeing some of the book bindings. She was a little reluctant to pull them off the shelves.

She resigned herself to sitting in the uncomfortable-looking chair. She sat stiffly, tapping her fingers restlessly on its wooden arms. Doing her best to look cooperative, she pasted a smile onto her face.

Amanda tried to maintain her composure when Jacob entered the room, but she couldn't hold back a shiver as his eyes locked onto hers.

"Beautiful," he stated, throwing his hands up, "simply stunning." Amanda guessed he meant her. "You're feeling better, I see." Amanda nodded, trying to seem pleased.

"Afraid to talk to me? Even after you promised to serve me for an eternity... I thought we were past that," he said, closing the gap between them and placing his hand on her shoulder.

It took every ounce of self-control not to pull away from his grasp.

Amanda spoke carefully, concentrating on keeping her voice steady. "Then why do I have this thing on my ankle?" She looked up to meet his gaze.

"I don't see how much trouble you could get into." He tightened his grip on her shoulder. "But my servant disagrees. He thinks we need to keep a close eye on you." Jacob gestured to the thick piece of metal with his free hand. "That enchanted shackle should serve as a reminder, Amanda, that you are my prisoner, unless I see fit to deem you otherwise." *Prison. Erol.*

Amanda let her smile drop and leaned forward in her chair. "Where is Erol? You have him here, don't you?"

"Ahh, worried about the jinn, are you?" He released her shoulder and grinned down at her. "I am keeping him far from you... for now. His prison, you might say, has been imprisoned." He chuckled. "I couldn't just let him keep gallivanting around in your dreams after all, could I?" He raised his eyebrows and

79

clicked his tongue. "Tsk, tsk Amanda, you couldn't possibly have expected me to trust you that easily." He strode menacingly around her chair. "You, on the other hand, don't have much of a choice; your fate is entirely up to me."

Amanda sat up in the chair. "What do you want from me, exactly?"

"I told you what I seek."

"What makes you think I can find it, if you could not? I'm sure you have been looking for this ring for a long time."

"I needed the right guide... and the right jinn to do the job. Why do you think?" Jacob leaned down close to Amanda's face as if inspecting her. His hot rancid breath invaded her nostrils; she wrinkled her nose and refused to breathe as he continued.

"Erol has been cursed for a long time. He was once in the service of the man to whom the ring was endowed. Until the man reached his final resting place, that is." He returned to his full, upright position, and Amanda allowed herself to breathe, emitting a gasp.

Jacob narrowed his eyes at her, and his voice rose as he added, "I will get the information from him one way or the other." He looked down at her, his cheeks now crimson. "You could be replaced, Amanda, but I think it would be a shame." He reached out and brushed his fingers against her cheek.

Amanda pressed her back into the chair and gripped its wooden arms tightly. Her heart raced.

"We could work well together, you know. From the moment I saw you I knew your heart was strong, but your will..." he leaned in toward her again, "is weak."

Amanda flinched and turned her face away.

"If you do choose to go back to my dungeon, just know that you will not find peace in death, no matter how long you starve and thirst. I will never let you perish completely. Just enough that Erol can move on to his next master."

Amanda turned her face back to Jacob, wide-eyed. "I thought I had to die for that to happen."

"Oh, there are ways to bring you to the brink of death, just enough." He paused, again searching her face. "Trust me, you do not want to know what that feels like. But if you are so curious, I can arrange it."

Amanda tightened her grip on the chair's arms, digging at them with her nails. "So why don't you just take over and get it yourself?"

"Erol, as you call him. It's funny that he would give you his real name. I wonder why he trusts you with that power?" He scratched at his chin. "I am the cause of his curse, it seems, and the one person who cannot be his master. At least not without the ring."

Well, at least I know why he needs someone else to control Erol. Amanda loosened her death grip. "When can I see him?"

"When you decide to truly cooperate... Now, let me show you some hospitality." He reached for her hand. "Dinner is waiting."

Amanda allowed him to pull her up from the chair. His cold hand felt rough against her fingers as he escorted her out of the library and farther down the stone corridor.

12

Jacob released her fingers as the corridor opened up into the dining area. Amanda couldn't help but wipe her hand across the fabric of her pant leg, trying to rid herself of the clammy feel of his skin.

Jacob didn't seem to notice as he sat at the end of the long wooden table that stretched the entire length of the room. The table could have seated fifty people easily, if not for the fact that there was only one other chair pushed beneath it.

The entire room seemed to be illuminated by the flickering light of a massive fireplace that had been dug into the far wall. The warm glow comforted Amanda. For a moment she was able to call up images of camping trips and roasting marshmallows as she stood still, breathing in the familiar scent of the burning pine.

But the old images were soon replaced by the newer, more intense memory of her childhood home as it burned, collapsing in front of her.

Amanda looked at Jacob as she felt a tear roll down her cheek. She clenched her teeth, trying to control her emotions.

Jacob smirked as he gestured for Amanda to sit. *He's enjoying this*, she thought as she moved toward the empty chair. Each step she took toward the seat echoed eerily in the otherwise empty room. She clutched the back of the chair, scraping it harshly against the stone floor as she pulled it out to take her seat. Amanda didn't know how much more of this she could take; *I am only human, after all.* She hid her shaky hands on her lap beneath the table. Taking slow shallow breaths, she willed them to be still.

Jacob muttered a few unintelligible sentences from his seat. The smell of burning pine was replaced by a new overwhelming aroma as a feast appeared before them. Amanda couldn't recall the last time she had eaten an actual meal, but she wasn't sure she could keep food down after what had just transpired.

Silver platters were piled high with chunks of poultry and beef. There were towers of buns and baked goods. Several bowls of fruits were arranged at the center of the table. They surrounded what appeared to be a large, cylindrical jelly sculpture that jiggled and swayed as Jacob stood and reached for a giant leg of poultry.

It all looked delicious, but her mind was still reeling with the things Jacob had said and done. Amanda wanted more answers—something important was missing. Some valuable key to her understanding.

"Well, Amanda, aren't you going to eat something?" She looked in Jacob's direction as he tore into a drumstick, ripping at the meat with his teeth. "Or have you lost your appetite?" He smiled as grease dribbled down his chin and hand.

Amanda forced a half smile and gave him a curt nod as she reached for a sticky bun. She pulled small pieces off and popped them into her mouth. The idea of things showing up out of nowhere still made her a bit hesitant. She swallowed the sweet chunks of bread, and her stomach growled at her with appreciation. Whether she wanted to eat or not, she needed to.

Amanda cleared her throat before she spoke. "Why isn't your ifrit here?"

Jacob didn't bother to swallow before speaking. "Why or how you ended up with such an affinity for these jinni, it perplexes me." He took a gulp of liquid from his chalice and belched.

"The jinn, unlike you and me, do not need food to survive. They enjoy it, yes, but they do not have to consume it as we do." He tore off another chunk of meat with his teeth and tossed the remains of the drumstick onto the table.

"You really need to learn more about your friends?" He smirked at her, his eyes wrinkling at the corners. "I only allow him food as a reward, and besides," Jacob wiped his face with the sleeve of his robe, "he has done nothing to earn a seat here with us. Especially since he saw fit to let you sever your ropes and eat the apples from the wisps, those vermin below."

Amanda gasped.

"Ah yes, puppet, I knew. Don't think me so foolish, or you won't last here long. Really, Amanda, you realize they are not like us." He shoved a hunk of bread into his mouth.

Amanda stared down at her plate; she could never let this vile man have the ring that he was seeking. She thought about what Erol had said in the dream. *If I ever want to get out of this alive, I have to do what he asks.* She nodded at Jacob and reached for some fruit.

The ifrit—there was no way he was happy to be serving this beast. She needed to earn the ifrit's trust if she was ever going to free herself and Erol. She popped a few grapes into her mouth and tapped her fingers on the table, lost in thought. She swallowed the fruit; still only half-chewed, it went down a little painfully. *Maybe it could work.* Amanda stood and stretched her arms up into the air. "Excuse me," she forced a yawn, "I am so tired."

Jacob looked up at her from his seat and grinned. Amanda could see green and brown food debris caught in his teeth. "Sweet dreams, puppet," he said, winking at her. Amanda reached across the table for a piece of fruit and threw him a quick smile. "For later?"

Jacob gestured toward the vast array, signaling her to go ahead. Amanda selected a ripe peach. She held it up to show him. Jacob nodded and made a shooing gesture. Amanda turned away from him to leave and rolled her eyes.

The ifrit was beside her then. *Has he been there all along? Watching?*

"Take her to her room," Jacob ordered.

Amanda gave the ifrit a slight curtsy and a smile. "Lead the way."

She followed closely behind him as he led her back through the corridor and up the winding staircase.

When they came to the door at the top, Amanda reached for him. He jerked away from her touch before she could position the piece of fruit into his hand. Bright flames danced in his eyes as she considered them.

"Payment for a name." She reached toward him again, and he backed up farther to the very edge of the landing. "It doesn't have to be your name, just something to call you." She smiled up at him, but he seemed unfazed.

She took another step forward and watched as once again he attempted to back up. His foot couldn't find the floor fast enough, and he began to stumble backward; he flailed his arms, trying to regain his footing. Amanda was ready and grabbed for him, yanking him toward her back onto the landing.

He stood still, eyeing her for a moment, before he reached out and grabbed the peach. "Call me what you wish."

"Hmm." Amanda tapped her fingers against the side of the wall, giggling to herself at the prospect of calling him Gene, as in Gene the Genie. She covered her grin and pushed the notion out of her head as he stared back at her with his cracked mouth set in a tight line.

"Okay, jinn are called fire spirits, right?" He nodded once, a distant look in his eyes. "How about Aden?" she offered, remembering it meant fire in some language or other, she had forgotten which. "It suits you, I think." Again, he nodded. "Aden, then, will you talk to me?" She offered her hand to him, and Aden accepted.

His skin transformed, taking on a more human tone and texture as she led him into the room. Although his eyes remained the color of emeralds, Amanda no longer wanted to jump from her skin at his glare. His voice as he finally spoke seemed gentler.

"And what else do you want from me?" He eyed her warily.

"Tell me about yourself," she asked, genuinely curious. Aden's dark hair now hung around his face. As he pushed it back from his forehead and sat on the floor, cross-legged, Amanda realized she had seen him before his appearance in the dungeon. "You're the young man from the field in my dream!" Eerily, he reminded her of Erol. Not in looks, but in mannerisms.

"I had no need to stay inside your father when he was asleep." He shrugged, looking at the floor. "Possessing humans is just as uncomfortable for me as for the person being controlled." Aden crossed his arms over his chest. "And it takes time to weaken a person, to control them fully and for longer periods."

"I know Jacob ordered you to do it, Aden." Amanda knelt beside him.

"Amanda, I have been here for a very long time." Aden stood, seeming annoyed with her questions. "There's really nothing more I am able to tell you."

Amanda looked up at him as she pushed herself back up off the floor. "Like your whole life? What are you, sixteen or seventeen?

Aden seemed to stare through Amanda as he continued. "Jinn do not age the same way humans do. I have been with the sorcerer for hundreds of years. Since I was a very young, it takes jinn that long to reach adolescence." Amanda was still trying to figure out what that meant as he added, "On top of being in the Arcane plane for most of the years, where time moves much more slowly than any of the other seven realms."

"Seven? Wait, where are we, Aden?"

His lips moved to a thin line. "We are in the Arcane plane, currently." He squinted as if he was in pain and furrowed his brow. "I have to go." He turned into white smoke that billowed out the door.

Amanda sat on the edge of her bed, trying to decide how to start a journey she had no hope of returning from. She had no idea how to prepare. *Maybe there is a questing for dummies book in the library?* She wondered what she was supposed to be doing, exactly, but decided it was time she found out. As she ventured from her room, the cold, hard metal of the shackle on her leg reminded her that she was not exactly free to do as she pleased.

13

On the day Amanda and Erol were to depart, she felt no closer to the answers she sought. Half of the books in the library were in languages she didn't understand.

The sorcerer brought out a box that seemed to have been constructed of iron. He produced a key from somewhere within his robes. The lock face had a skull carved into it, and Jacob inserted the key into its mouth and turned. As Jacob lifted the lid on the heavy iron box, Amanda could see runes drawn on the inside of the lid that glowed faintly. They looked quite similar to the ones on the dagger blade and sheath.

From it he pulled the lamp. It had been hidden inside surrounded by the iron, which she had heard from Erol was poison to a jinni. The magic runes, she had no doubt, had blocked him from coming to her aid and to her dreams.

Her heart skipped a beat at the sight of the lamp.

Amanda bit down on her tongue to keep herself from smiling as Erol appeared from his prison. Erol turned to her and addressed her. "Hello, mistress." His lips formed a straight, tight line as he bowed.

Did my emotions crash into him immediately upon his release from the double prison, hitting him like a wave? It's just an act, Amanda. "My servant," Amanda addressed him. She had to concentrate so she did not blush as he eyed her attire. She had only known him a short time before she was kidnapped by the sorcerer but realized how terribly she had missed the company he gave.

Amanda shivered slightly as Erol put his arm around her waist.

"Leaving already?" Jacob interrupted. "You know where to find what I seek, then?" He raised his eyebrows. "Because I know you are aware that there is no use in trying to run."

"No." Erol shook his head. "But I have an idea of where to start."

"Well, get on with it then, my dear puppets." Jacob made a shooing motion.

"Are you ready, mistress?" Amanda nodded. "This will be a little different than how we traveled before. Hold on to my hand and walk with me." Amanda grasped his free hand.

A breeze suddenly pushed past them, and Erol turned toward it and stepped. The wind lifted them, swirling and dancing around their bodies as they walked together from the run-down castle. The sprawling building with its plain rectangular body and single tower would not have been impressive on its own, but Amanda's grip loosened on Erol's hand as she took in the sight that surrounded the castle.

The sorcerer's home had been constructed beside a mountain that seemed to stretch all the way up into the clouds. Several ledges jutted out above the length of the castle and tower. A constant flow of water from somewhere above these ledges cascaded down, creating a waterfall that surrounded the fortress.

Erol whispered into her ear, "Don't look down and don't let go."

Places and people seemed to pass by them and through them in a blur. Amanda's heart raced with excitement; she decided immediately that she enjoyed wind-walking.

When the swirling stopped, brown, vast, endless desert speckled with rolling hills stretched out before them. Sweat instantly began to form on Amanda's face from the merciless yellow sun overhead.

"Erol," she said now that they were away from Jacob's eyes and ears. She put her arms around him and hugged him tightly. Erol placed his arm across her back in return; he grinned.

"Nice clothes."

Amanda felt her face heat up. She had forgotten about the clothing. For just a moment, she had even forgotten that they were not free of the sorcerer's grasp.

"We need to make haste with our journey. Many of the Arcane, like Jacob, still thirst for jinn blood. They just aren't willing to go to the measures he has taken, but if we are going to present ourselves on a silver platter..." He shrugged.

"Then why risk it, Erol?"

"I need some information. But we must be careful. Even if Jacob is not present at this moment, he will have eyes on us." Erol eyed her up and down again.

"Ah, Amanda," he joked. "As striking as you do look in the skintight clothing, here." He thrust a heavy woolen robe her way. The material felt coarse as she slid it on over her clothing, and she wondered if she would melt from the afternoon's heat.

"Put the hood up. Some in this land will be able to see my true nature. We don't want to attract any unwanted attention." Amanda did as he asked, and Erol was also soon covered by the thick fabric of a similar robe. "We will be fine once we get to the palace. We will need to walk from here."

Amanda's feet felt heavy as they reached the top of a dune. Before them, a short way ahead in the distance, stood several white rectangular buildings protruding up out of the sand. People covered in heavy robes like their own walked chestnut horses through the encrusted paths.

In the center rose a huge square palace with a domed top. Amanda gaped in awe at the massive structure; she had never seen anything like it in person. *It's one of the most beautiful things I have ever set my eyes on.*

"How are we supposed to blend in here?" Amanda whispered.

"Shhh."

Amanda followed close behind Erol as they strolled through the market area, her heart pounding. Each time the merchants turned to them, holding up linen and clothes, metal trinkets, and loaves of bread, her breath caught in her throat. It felt like an eternity had passed before they managed to push through the bustling place.

Amanda's hands were shaking as they approached the palace. She let out a sigh of relief at the thought of getting out of the crowd and the noise.

Several men wearing white uniforms lined the entrance. "What business do you have here?" one of them bellowed as Erol began ascending the steps. He stretched out his muscular arm to block their path. His skin looked weathered; a scar ran from just below his eye down to his chin.

Erol gestured to Amanda to remain where she was. The guard cast a skeptical look at Erol as he pushed his hood back, revealing his face. The guard lowered his arm, and Erol continued toward him slowly, speaking to him in a language Amanda could not understand. After a moment Erol gestured for her to follow.

The marble floor beneath her feet glistened as they were directed into a marvelous hall. The ceiling must have been twenty feet high. Amanda pushed back her hood, in awe of her surroundings. There was a large black brazier in the center of the room. Vases of fascinating design lined the walls. Wide-eyed, Amanda studied the tiny, detailed pictures that had been hand-painted on each one.

A man Amanda assumed could only be the ruler was seated across the room on a throne of golden hue. The edges of his chair were embedded with rubies and gems. Every inch of his exposed skin seemed to be covered with colorful tattoos. As Amanda neared the throne, she stifled a giggle at the single bushy bar that resided above his seemingly unblinking eyes.

Erol got down on the floor and kissed in between the man's feet, so Amanda mimicked his actions. Again, Erol spoke in the strange language as he stood and bowed before the man. The man rose from his seat, narrowing his eyes as he responded. Amanda was completely lost trying to follow the strange tongue as he and Erol spoke together. She tried to stay still but couldn't help looking around admiringly at her surroundings.

There was a faint whoosh as a fire lit, seemingly on its own, in the brazier. Then, as if enthralled, Amanda started moving gracefully toward it. Her feet had taken on a mind of their own. She heard the conversation trail off as her body swayed back and forth and around in a strange dance to music that she could not hear with her ears. The song seemed to play from inside her.

"Amanda?" Erol reached toward her to follow. Amanda turned her head back toward him but was unable to stop herself from moving as she continued around the fire.

The man plopped back down onto his elegant throne, and an amused look spread across his face as he watched Amanda's dance.

"What a pretty slave you have got there," came a shrill voice, seemingly from nowhere.

Amanda watched as Erol's face turned crimson. He furrowed his brow and squinted his eyes into slits as a man stepped out from behind some curtains.

Amanda thought she heard a hint of desperation in Erol's voice as he addressed the white-haired man that had appeared. "Bloise, please stop playing your games. We come about an urgent matter." Amanda was only able to catch glimpses of his silvery robes as she continued to sway around the room.

Amanda was becoming dizzy with her movements. "Erol?" she questioned, wanting the room to stop spinning.

"I know exactly why you have come. Am I not the most powerful wizard alive? Why do you think I would help a jinni and a girl?" He gestured to the ruler. "I think you should take them to the dungeon and leave them to rot, Your Majesty." Bloise bowed toward the king.

The ruler clapped his hands, and several guards came into the room. Amanda screamed as they grabbed at her arms, her dance finally ending, her heart pounding as she kicked out her feet, trying to stop them from dragging her away. She looked around as they pulled her. Erol did not seem to be protesting as the guards tugged at him. They led them down several flights of stairs and shoved them through some curtains.

As the guards released their hold, Amanda was slightly relieved at the realization that they were not in fact being thrown into a dungeon. This was someone's living quarters. Colorful cloths were draped over every wall. A large, round bed and wide wardrobe took up one side of the room. The rest of the space was unfurnished but contained a multitude of large pillows that were placed about the floor, seemingly at random.

"There is no reason to look for a way out," Erol said as he crossed his legs beneath himself and sat on the floor. "The wizard, Bloise, just likes the ruler to believe he is still in charge."

"I wasn't." Her voice cracked as she spoke.

"Amanda, even if I could not feel your emotions, I would still know you were lying. You're not very good at it."

"What do you mean? The sorcerer believed me, didn't he," Amanda replied angrily.

"You really believe he trusts you?" Erol questioned, his arms folded in front of him.

Amanda looked away. "Well, who should I trust then?" She emphasized the *I*.

"No one."

"Why are we here? I think I should know."

"The city? To get information. This room? I think I have information this wizard could use."

"How do you know that he won't kill me and take you then?"

"I don't think that's what Bloise is after, Amanda." Erol kicked at a pillow on the floor. "He has no need for me. He is older and more powerful than any I have encountered before."

"So he can stop Jacob then?"

"No, that mess is for us. He won't get so involved in our affairs, but he does have information he might be willing to exchange with me."

The white-haired wizard entered then, accompanied by several smiling women dressed in brightly colored sheer fabrics.

Dimples appeared on Bloise's cheeks as he grinned. "Introductions?" Crow's feet radiated from the corners of his eyes.

Erol shook his head. "You already know our names."

"No need to be grouchy. I was just having fun, lad."

"Well, you scared Amanda." Erol puffed out his chest.

"Oh relax, she's fine, aren't you girly?" He winked at her. "I borrowed that bit of magic straight from the realm of the goddesses. It's something new, I think." His eyes danced with excitement. "Could you imagine a being with the ability to control others just with the sound of her song?"

"I thought you vowed never to 'borrow' magic again?" Erol said, pursing his lips. "And that's crazy. The sisters haven't been able to create new beings since they divided the realms."

"Well, maybe they have learned a thing or two in the last few hundred thousand years. I tell you something's coming. I can feel it in my old bones. Something far worse than old Jacob. I plan to be prepared."

He gestured toward Amanda.

"Take her to be cleaned up a bit. She reeks of travel and of jinn." He turned to Erol and opened his mouth. "Wait." He turned back to Amanda. "His talisman, so he may remain here for a talk with me." Boise held out a wrinkled hand toward her. Erol nodded to her in approval, and Amanda reached beneath her garment, where she had secured it in the layer of heavy but loose cloth.

"I can do it myself," Amanda grunted, taking the ivory brush from one of the girls that had been attempting to style her now-snarled blonde hair. She examined the head of the brush, tracing the outline with her fingers. The unbristled side had been carved into the shape of an elephant's head, and the handle represented the trunk. Amanda ran it through her hair a few times.

It was bad enough that Bloise's servants would not leave the room; they had forcefully helped her change clothing. Amanda looked at herself in the mirror. Her face turned a bright crimson at the sight. *What exactly are this wizard's intentions?* From the scanty way these handmaidens had dressed her, she assumed the worst. The shirt looked more like a bikini top, and the silk pants were cut several inches below her navel and rested on her hips. Amanda felt exposed. The handmaidens approached her again, this time carrying several silver boxes with all kinds of jewelry and one rather large needle.

Amanda backed away in protest, accidentally bumping into one woman, knocking her box from her hands and sending glinting pieces of jewelry flying in all directions. There was no way she was letting them pierce her skin with that thing. Seeing the rest of the handmaidens set their boxes carefully upon the floor to try to pick up the jewels, Amanda took her chance to run for the door. There was a reason she had no piercings. She did not like needles at all. She would rather take her chances with the wrath of the wizard.

She could overhear their conversation as she got nearer to the room where she had left Erol.

"...Blood is a rare commodity," Bloise proclaimed.

"You're sure?"

"You must tell her."

"You'll frighten her; she is hanging by a thread."

"What stops me from keeping her for myself then? She is too weak to fulfill the duty you need her to."

"You will push her over the edge, wizard."

"She could be used for aid in a few spells, and you can go about this quest of yours. Someone like her is hard to come by in these times."

"Everybody has a dark side, and I do not think I would want to awaken hers, if what you say is true. One can only imagine the power she would have if she went the other way. And if it was by your hand... Amanda, you return."

"I don't like needles," she said, glaring at Bloise, trying not to let on that she had heard a thing as she entered the room.

"Hmm, pity," the wizard replied, looking Amanda up and down.

Amanda crossed her arms over her belly, trying to hide herself from his scrutiny. Erol picked up a long shawl that had been strewn across a chair and walked toward her with it. He said, "Really, wizard, and how will we leave the city with her looking so?" He handed Amanda the shawl and gestured in her direction.

"Travel as jinn do to the place I told you about. You will find no humans there, so it is not of real concern." Bloise started out of the room, then turned sharply back. "Don't forget your promise to me, jinn." Erol nodded, and the wizard disappeared around the corner, grinning from ear to ear.

Embarrassed, Amanda stepped farther from Erol and wrapped the shawl around her shoulders, trying to cover as much skin as possible.

"We must go back to the human realm," Erol said. Stepping back toward Amanda, he hesitated momentarily as he started to wrap his arm around her waist, this time touching her bare skin and sending a shiver across it. Like the times before, in her living room and in the cellar, the scene around them shifted and fell away.

14

When they emerged, a few wispy clouds could be seen overhead in the bright blue sky, but the land was barren. Amanda saw no other living things. It was deathly quiet.

Erol turned her chin gently toward him. "I wanted to be sure." He considered her eyes.

"Sure of what?" Erol broke eye contact with her and looked out into the barren landscape. "Well, where are we then?" Amanda asked, glad to be back on firm ground. The ground beneath her was dark and musty. It was hard to breathe in the thick, stale air.

"The tomb of a great man," he responded as he lit a torch and looked about at the gray and brown stone walls.

"The tomb of a dead person?" Amanda had a bad taste in her mouth at the thought.

"Who else is a tomb for?" he responded. "Don't worry; I do not think we need to speak to him."

"Wait, I thought you couldn't bring dead people back."

"That doesn't mean I can't speak to them, does it?" He lifted a torch from the wall, and it burst into flames. "The magic that emanates here is said to attract lost items and hidden knowledge."

"So you think the ring is here?"

"No, the ring isn't lost, it's hidden, but there is a jinni here that may be able to help."

Amanda saw a glint in the sand-colored floor and bent down to see a familiar palm-sized black diamond. The last time she had laid her eyes on it had been when Erol gave it to her. She snatched it up and put it in her pocket without much thought.

Amanda looked around. The space wasn't wide but appeared rather lengthy, spreading outward like endless tunnels on each side of her. It reminded her of the gloom of the dungeon. Amanda turned in a circle; she couldn't see Erol anywhere.

She reached into her pocket and caressed the jewel, trying to decide which direction he had disappeared toward. The hair on her neck prickled. She took a slow, deep breath. *He can't just leave me.* She took another breath. *He has to be right around here somewhere.*

Amanda stomped her foot in frustration. Something landed in her hair from above, crawling down her back. She swatted at the thing and shook off her clothing. A fist-sized eight-legged creature landed at her feet and scurried away. She rubbed her bare arms at the thought of the thing that had been crawling on her. Why did she have to come to this dirty, disgusting tomb? She caressed the jewel in one hand and squeezed her other hand into a tight fist. Why had he brought her here? She wanted to scream.

"Erol," she yelled, even though she knew it wasn't necessary. *He has to be right here somewhere.*

As he appeared, he looked quizzically at her.

"Why did you do this to me? I am your boss, not the other way around. How dare you." Rage filled her. She wanted to hurt him as he had hurt her. Taking her only family from her. Causing her all this pain. She touched the scars on her back, remembering what she had endured.

"I can see and feel you're upset, but I'm not sure... Amanda, what did you do?"

There was fear in his voice, and Amanda liked the way it made her feel, like she had power over him. She felt like a storm was brewing inside of her. She glared at him, her fists now at her side.

The force pushing inside of her built, unable to escape. *Do I want it to?* Amanda wanted him to feel the way she had when she had been alone and helpless. But she held it at bay. *Maybe if a little escapes, I won't feel like I am going to explode from the inside. Just a little won't hurt.* Amanda pushed it out, away from Erol.

The floor shook beneath her; she heard canisters and jars crashing as the rumble caused them to fall from the stone shelves. The heavy stone lid cracked across the top of the rectangular resting place, letting a glimmer of light shine in.

Erol looked around, confused. Amanda wasn't sure she could stop. She could tell the power was somehow coming from her. She saw Erol grimace and stumble as the angry force overtook her.

Erol grabbed at her shoulder and started shaking her. "You will bring this whole place down on our heads," he warned. The jewel fell from her hand.

Amanda crumpled to the floor.

Erol reached out and touched the jewel then pulled his hand back as if it had bitten him. Amanda sat up rubbing the back of her skull; she felt the jewel still pulsing with power even now.

A voice squeaked from the shadows. "Why would you bring that poor girl here? Some servant you are." Mischief danced in the newcomer's unusual yellow eyes. She had waist-long brown hair, which swayed from side to side as she approached.

"I was looking for you." Erol looked away, ashamed. "We need some information from you." The jinni crinkled her nose.

She reached down and pushed the jewel into a small drawstring bag. She lifted the bag by its strings and held it out away from herself before she responded. "Oh, I know what information you seek." She eyed Erol. "They will never let you have the ring."

"If we don't bring it to Jacob, he will just find someone else to do it; he won't stop until he gets what he wants one way or another."

"If you say so." She smirked.

"This isn't just about him enslaving the jinn; I think he has bigger plans."

"Oh, I know exactly what he's after. You are the one that has no idea," the jinn female said, frowning. "I can tell you I have looked after this place a long time; the ring has never resided here with its original master."

She kneeled by Amanda, looking her over, before adding, "It's said it was taken by another upon his death. I believe it was given to a jinni guardian, to be sure it would never fall into the wrong hands again." She lifted the bag. "Here." She thrust it toward Amanda. "It's yours, that's why you found it here." Amanda took the bag. The jinn faded before even all her words could be heard. "Maybe it will help, but be sure you don't use it until you need to."

"Are you okay?" Erol asked, reaching a hand down to help Amanda up.

"What happened?"

Erol put his arm around her as she wobbled on her feet.

Amanda opened the top of the bag and looked at the diamond only for a moment, then pulled it shut. "Is this what caused all this?" She looked around the room, evaluating the destruction of what should have been a peaceful resting place, gesturing all around.

"You and it, yes, we may need it."

"I don't think I can, Erol." She held the bag out to him. "It was calling to me from my pocket, begging me to hold it, to touch it. I couldn't stop myself. I don't want it."

"Amanda, you are stronger than that thing. You just need to learn how to use it to your advantage."

"It sure didn't feel like it." She rubbed her bare arms as if chilled. "It felt like it was stronger than me."

"You have more inside than you know, Amanda."

Amanda's stomach felt like lead. "The feeling scared me, and it should scare you too."

"You would never hurt anyone on purpose." He touched her arm lightly.

"How do you know, because I don't even know anymore. I wanted to. Erol, I wanted to hurt you!" she yelled.

Erol wrapped her in his arms and held her close, trying to calm her. He considered her eyes and leaned in toward her as if he expected a kiss. Amanda pulled away with all her strength. Erol looked back at her, hurt apparent in his gaze. A frown on his lips, he grabbed on to her and the world shifted and melted away.

"Here we are, Amanda rest here." Erol gestured to the field that spread out before them.

A sense of relief washed over her. He had brought her to the place under the tree she had dreamed about so many times. "Erol, is this place real or not?"

"It's real, Amanda."

"I have actually eaten apples like these before." She gestured to the few pieces of fruit on the ground under the tree.

"In one of your dreams?"

"No, the wisps or whatever they were gave them to me when I was imprisoned."

"Wisps?"

Amanda described the glowing balls to him and their behavior, how they seemed scared of her and yet seemed to be watching over her at the same time.

He sat then with a strange expression. "I am not all-knowing, Amanda. Although I have been around a long time, things are always changing, and there is still much I have not seen. As you have witnessed, there are other planes besides mine and yours. There are places where the different plans meet and converge slightly." He ran his fingers through his hair. "Those runes Jacob carved into your back, they are the symbols for the seven planes. It's like he already knew we..." he stammered a bit, "like he already knew you would need to travel to my home plane to get the ring, and he was starting to prepare you for it."

"What do you mean?"

"The realms were created to keep us from our wars with each other. To separate us. The jinni and the Arcane, mainly. And to keep the humans safe."

"You're doing a bad job explaining again," she whispered in a sleepy voice.

"The point is, it's not easy to jump from realm to realm. It's not meant to be done. It takes strong magic to do it once, let alone multiple times."

Amanda rested her head on his shoulder; she felt him tense up rigidly beside her. "We have to get back," he said stiffly.

"Let's just rest for a moment," Amanda said, closing her eyes; she ran her fingers through his hair. After a moment he seemed to give in and relax.

Erol jumped up suddenly, causing Amanda to fall over. An orange and red light danced in the distance. No, it wasn't dancing, it was moving toward them. The orange blur started to take shape.

"It's him," Erol spat. "He has come to check on us."

"How could he find us here?"

"I told you the sorcerer has ways to find us. He has sent his bully for us."

"He is not a bully," Amanda responded sharply, with renewed energy. She surprised herself at how defensive she sounded.

"No, well, remember, jinn have free will, and to be what he is now, he must have done some pretty bad things."

"He was made to do them. His free will was taken from him," she retorted.

"Amanda, I forget how young and naive you are." He grabbed for her hand. "He could have chosen to let the sorcerer destroy him."

Amanda pulled away from his grasp. "And is that what I should have chosen, Erol?" She was practically shouting.

Aden chuckled as he now stood right in front of her. "Stopped to have a spat?"

Amanda ignored Aden. "You don't know what happened to him," she continued to address Erol.

Aden interrupted. "Oh, he knows, Amanda. He knows much more than he lets on." Aden looked him up and down.

"Shut up," Erol responded, shoving Aden.

Aden grabbed at Erol's shirt. "You're not powerful enough to make me, Erol." He balled his free hand at his side.

"Both of you stop," Amanda shouted. "Geesh, boys, and my dad wondered why I never wanted to date. I'm not going to be a part of this." She stomped away from them; they could argue on their own. Amanda pretended to be interested in the flowers on the far side of them; their voices continued to carry to her on the wind, just as they had in her dreams.

"Aden, if that's what you're calling yourself now?" Erol questioned. Amanda watched from a distance as he folded his arms in front of himself.

"She picked it. Does it make you jealous?" Aden smirked. Amanda leaned down as if she were sniffing the flowers, curious where this conversation would lead; she still needed answers.

"She would never want someone like you. Have you even told her any of the shameful things you have done?" Erol pointed at Aden's chest.

"If you say so, Erol, but once you fail her just like you failed me, who will she turn to?"

"I was helpless." Amanda's heart beat faster in her chest at Erol's words.

"No, you weren't paying attention," Aden yelled. "It was your duty!"

Amanda's ears perked up. She closed her eyes and breathed in deeply as something dawned on her. She had to be sure.

They were so busy arguing, they didn't even seem to notice as she began to approach them, purposefully only moving a few feet at a time.

Erol leaned in close to Aden's face and whispered, "Bloise said not to interfere. She will make the right choice." *Doesn't he realize I can still hear him?* "Needs to make the right choice." Erol looked down at his feet. "I will tell her as promised…"

Amanda made her final move toward them. "We aren't getting any rest here. We might as well just go," she said. Neither would look at her. Amanda pushed past both and stood between them.

"Wait." Another thought occurred to her. "Aden, why can you travel so far from the knife? And we are stuck together like glue?" She pointed to Erol.

Aden raised his eyebrows and winked at Erol. "See? She is sick of you already."

Erol glared at Aden and balled his hands into fists. "That is part of my punishment, whereas he is being held by a different type of magic."

That answer seemed to satisfy her as she took Erol by the arm and wrapped it around her waist, almost surprising herself. "Alright, let's go." Her head was spinning with information.

15

"You came for me."

Erol, how can you be in my dream? she thought. They were still in the field, but the sky was dark. There were blue lightning bugs swarming the flowers. *No, not lightning bugs.* It was the wisps.

And then Amanda was being shaken again.

"She has traveled too many times today," Erol hissed. "Even with your runes, humans are not meant to swoosh around, hopping planes. It's too much for them."

"She will be fine." The sorcerer's gruff voice was unmistakable. Amanda wasn't sure she wanted to open her eyes.

"You sent him for us. What do you want? We are doing all we can," Erol shouted.

"Don't get lippy with me; I will encase you in iron again," Jacob countered.

"Suit yourself. I can't help her do your deeds then, at least," Erol replied. Amanda opened one of her eyes just enough to see their outlines above her.

"It has come to my attention that she needs to travel with you to the emerald mountains." Jacob turned to Erol. "Only I can teach her the secret."

"I will go alone," Erol said.

"You cannot pass far enough into the plane without her, and you know it," Jacob bellowed.

Amanda opened her eyes then. "Teach me what?"

"Oh my dearest, there you go, see, she is fine." The sorcerer winked at her.

"Yeah, like you were real worried," Erol retorted.

"I shall teach you how to get into the plane where you will be able to find the relic we seek."

"Where's Aden?" questioned Amanda. Her head was pounding.

"There is no need for his presence," the sorcerer replied. "Unless of course, you wish it." He smiled slyly.

"Outrageous," Erol responded. "Why would she?"

Grinning, the sorcerer replied, "You know nothing of her true heart, Erol." He poked Erol's chest.

"I know everything I need to know," he responded matter-of-factly.

Amanda decided she better drop it. "What's with all the arguing? Let's just get this over with so he can take over everyone's free will already." She surprised herself with how uncaring she sounded. She wondered if that really was how she felt; she was so confused lately. Erol looked at her with his mouth half open. Amanda turned away, letting Erol's relic slide out of her grasp. She marched off, leaving Erol with Jacob.

She changed into a short black top and skirt. The boots had been replaced by another almost identical pair, and she put those on. She checked herself out in the mirror; she was getting used to the way these clothes clung to her. She smiled at her reflection.

"Hello, beautiful!"

Startled, Amanda turned to see Aden behind her; she had forgotten how Erol hadn't cast a reflection in her mirror.

"How long have you been watching me in here?"

"Only a moment. Might I say how lovely you do look." He placed his hand lightly on her cheek and moved it softly down to her chin.

She stepped back from his touch. "Aden, I need answers."

"The truth is in front of you, Amanda; you don't want to see it." Aden looked around the room. "There are just so many things I am unable to say. I have to tell you what I can." Aden looked into her eyes. "I asked Jacob to give your father the dagger." His shoulders slumped. "I told him he would give in to me easier if we gave him what he was searching for."

Amanda took a step back. "I don't understand."

"I thought maybe one of you would break the seal and release me. Jacob knew I didn't have a way to do it myself, but I thought..." Aden paused, looking around the room again. "I just wanted you to know."

The door flew open, banging against the stone wall with the sudden force; the sorcerer tossed Erol's prison onto the floor.

Startled again, Amanda searched the room with her eyes. Aden had vanished.

"Don't bring this back down with you. I have had all I can take from that foolish jinni today. You should put him in his place, my dear."

"Yes," she replied before she could stop herself as he exited, slamming the door.

Amanda jumped as a hand grasped her shoulder. She spun around. "You two have to stop doing that," she said as she took in Erol's form.

"You two? Who else has been... oh." Erol looked angry. Amanda swore she saw fire in his eyes for just a moment, but then it was gone.

"Amanda, be careful," he said, grasping her hand. "I don't want anything happening to you."

"Don't you think," Amanda pulled her hand away, "it's a little late to be worried about that?" She turned and stomped out of the room.

"Ah, precious, you come, at last, to learn. I thought I was going to have to wait all night."

"Will Aden be joining us?"

"No, stop being concerned for Aden. He never enjoyed the power I helped him achieve. Soon I will be done with him entirely.

Not like you will, Amanda. You enjoy it already, I can tell."

Amanda looked away. Was it true? There was something dark growing inside of her; she wasn't sure if she would be able to crawl back to the light.

Jacob gestured to her. "Sit; I need you to read these. The process cannot be explained in words." He spoke what sounded like gibberish and waved his hands over her.

"What are you doing?" she demanded.

"This language is a secret, the only language the jinn cannot understand. Maybe you should learn a little more about your friends, the jinni as well," he said, tossing a small, delicate book onto the carved desk. "You will only have one chance in and one chance out, so do not mess up." Amanda took a seat on the uncomfortable wooden chair. "You could get stuck in that plane forever."

Jacob turned back as he was leaving. "Thank Erol for me when you get the chance."

She looked up from the desk. "Thank him?"

"For leading me straight to you, dear." He strode out the door.

16

Amanda picked up the smaller book. Nothing was written on its soft, leathery brown cover. She flipped it open at random. *What is this made from?* The paper was covered with a flurry of black ink; lines of handwritten word tumbled down the page. *Who could have handwritten on this delicate material. Could it be another spell of some sort?* The surface of the paper felt waxy beneath her fingers.

In the beginning, our universe was a vast, empty void. This void, it is said, contained space for endless worlds. One day out of the void emerged two powerful celestial beings, Eaki and Aya.

They had traveled from another universe in search of a place where there was room for their godlike children to grow. *Some strange mythology lesson?* Something her father would have read to her when she was a child, had he been fortunate enough to stumble upon it. Amanda trembled slightly at the memory.

How many similar tales of creation had she heard at bedtime when she was a young girl? *How is this supposed to help?* Amanda sighed. *My father would have been drawn to the mystery within the legend, enthralled by the words.* She read on.

They had brought with them the knowledge of creation and set about molding a simple world to live together in the center of the universe.

One by one, as their children were born, Eaki and Aya raised them to adolescence. Knowing at this age their children would begin to become restless and crave a deeper purpose, they sent them out into this universe to create a single world of their own to cultivate and control. They were each given a limited number of enchanted supplies to use. This is how our sun, our moons, and each unique planet came into existence.

Amanda turned the brittle page, and the thin paper made a crinkling noise between her fingers.

So it went until Aya gave birth to triplet daughters, Sophia, the firstborn, Akila the middle daughter, and Mia, the youngest. The two younger siblings bickered constantly and fought for their parents' attention. As the girls neared adolescence, their competitive nature only grew worse.

Her eyes flitted across the page. Words appeared and disappeared as she became immersed.

Sophia overheard Eaki and Aya discussing her two younger sisters and was troubled to hear that they doubted the girls would be able to sustain their creations for long.

The character leapt out at her, and she could picture herself standing just far enough away to remain unnoticed, as she had in the shop and at the field, straining to listen to words she wasn't supposed to hear.

When the time came, Eaki gave them each a chunk of enchanted clay, seeds, and some drops of his celestial blood. He sent them into the universe to create their individual worlds.

Sophia followed her sisters, and watching them bicker and fight, she decided that they could not be trusted to fulfill their father's wishes.

Amanda frowned, looking up from the page. *What would my father's wishes have been? Would I be strong enough to fulfill them?*

He would want me to learn all I could.

Determined to help them succeed and make her father proud, she persuaded them to combine the resources to create one larger, more diverse world together so they could share equally in the responsibilities.

Could I be strong enough to make my father proud?

Akila and Mia eagerly handed over the halves of their clay that was meant to be the base for their three small worlds. Sophia lumped the pieces of clay together and carefully started to shape the world. As she worked, the younger sisters teased and tormented one another.

Amanda's eyes wandered to the next page, ready to see more.

Sophia was content with the intelligent beings that she created and enjoyed watching them learn and progress.

What? She went back and read the last sentence. Her fingers traced the center binding. As she had expected, there was a thin rough line between the sheets where a page had been removed. *Why?* There was no telling how old the book could be. Her father would have had an idea. He would have been able to estimate its age just by the odd materials used to create it, how it smelled of dust, the unique writing inside. Amanda breathed in deeply, calming herself, and returned to the story.

Mia and Akila also watched the humans. Although the people were quite intelligent, they appeared weak to Mia and Akila. The sisters decided they would each make a magical race and have a contest between them to determine which of the two could create the most powerful beings.

Akila created the elemental spirits, the jinn, born of smokeless fire.

In response, Mia created beings with great arcane magic and taught them to hate the jinn and to pursue them relentlessly.

As the two races fought, Sophia's race of humans was often caught in the middle. Not having natural magic themselves, they were unable to put up an adequate defense.

Amanda's heart raced as she read on. She felt drawn to Sophia's plight and was eager to hear how she had solved her problem.

Sophia couldn't bear to see her humans so abused, and she jumped down onto the plate of land, splitting it into several pieces and spreading them apart across the vast seas that she had created. Hoping to spare her human race from future devastation, she placed them all onto one of the masses of land.

Amanda imagined the protector of the human race, the goddess Sophia, to be a radiant creature, her skin glowing, her body clad in crude armor, leaping down in rage and cracking the land with her fury,

Akila and Mia continued to pit their creations against one another, but it became apparent that the two species were somewhat equally matched.

Still, craving victory, Akila used the last of her clay to create beings of pure light and energy.

In response, Mia created demons of pure darkness, able to harness the shadows.

Do any of these other creatures live in the realms I have visited? Have I encountered them unknowingly? Surely they wouldn't have been able to hide among humans the way the Arcane and the jinn could... Amanda poured herself over the page, almost in a trance.

Again the sisters sent their creations on a path of destruction.

By this time, all being intelligent and curious species, they had discovered various ways to travel the great seas. Once again, the humans were thrust into a war they had no chance of surviving. Sophia scolded her sisters for being so careless as she watched her creation brought to the brink of extinction.

Sophia had been frightened for her creations. She wasn't afraid of what she had to do; she knew she had to be strong to protect them. *Could I be as strong as her?*

Still, the sisters ignored Sophia's plea's to stop their vicious campaign. The battles raged on until only two humans remained. Sophia's anger grew, and she was filled with rage at the destruction of the creations she had worked so hard on.

Sophia ripped and shredded the very fabric of the world, tearing each race away from the other and separating them into five different planes.

The story ended abruptly. Amanda tested the jagged edges of the missing pages with her fingers. Someone in the distant past had removed them. *For what purpose? To keep the past a secret, or the future?* Amanda wondered about the origin of the journal-like book as she examined the worn binding.

She flipped through its pages again and let a sigh escape her. *Another pointless game Jacob is playing with me.* She thought of how the book had immediately made her think of her father and how she had been drawn into Sophia's plight, as if she were a kindred spirit.

She pushed the book away, disgusted with the idea of being led astray again by the sorcerer.

She hesitated as she reached for one of the thick texts Jacob had placed on the desk. *What if it's not another lie? What if the information inside really is important? No.* Amanda shook her head and opened the much heavier book. *No, there's not enough time for nonsense.* Erol and Aden had made it clear that there were seven realms and seven races. Amanda was sure the missing pages were no more than a ruse created by Jacob to get her to question her friends. Clearly this was another false journey he was leading her on, *another wild goose chase...*

It was often hard to concentrate as she began. Her thoughts swirled, and she kept returning to what the sorcerer had said and the way the boys had been arguing. Amanda had practically memorized the two heavy volumes the sorcerer had given her before she first chose a book at random from the shelves, hoping to find a way to help Erol, Aden, and herself.

17

Dozens of flickering candles illuminated the stone walls. A constant draft caused the flames to dance, casting shadows all around, but the ebb and flow of light did nothing to distract Amanda from her task. She found she had become somewhat accustomed to the dimly lit rooms of the castle and those constantly moving shadows against every wall.

Amanda barely bothered to leave the library as the days passed. The room soon became her sanctuary; delving into the books allowed her to forget the things she had lost as she buried her memories behind a wall of information, focusing on her mission. Stopping Jacob and freeing his captives had become her obsession, her purpose.

She sat in silence at the rough wooden desk, studying the texts.

Amanda came to a page that spoke of releasing jinn from a sorcerer's power and greedily tried to absorb the information. *No.* She closed the book in disgust and sighed. *That is not the kind of release I am looking for.* She massaged her temples, frustrated. *I have to keep looking.* The sorcerer would be expecting her to be ready any time now. There had to be a spell that could allow her to free the jinn without someone having to die.

The quick movement as she stood caused the metal ring around her ankle to bite painfully at her flesh. *I am their only hope,* she reminded herself. Turning to the shelves of books that lined the walls, Amanda searched in desperation, scanning them for anything that seemed like it could be helpful.

A heavy volume, one with runes delicately carved into the cover, caught her eye. She hefted it from the shelf. Someone had handcrafted the cover and spine from some type of wood. She touched the runes lightly. She had definitely seen these particular symbols somewhere. *Before I was brought here?* A sapling of some type, still sprouting from its seed, had been whittled into the front. Amanda traced over the runes with her fingers.

As she moved to carry the book to the desk for a better look, the floor seemed to move slightly beneath her. The book dropped from her hand with a dull thud as the wave of dizziness intensified. She reached out, grabbing for the back of her chair to steady herself, and slid slowly downward until she felt the uncomfortable wooden seat beneath her.

Amanda closed her eyes, trying to focus on the familiar sounds around her. She listened for the rush of the waterfall that cascaded down outside the castle walls and took a deep breath, waiting for the spinning to stop. "One... two... three... four..." She counted each breath and released them in a slow deliberate fashion.

As the movement around her slowed, the sound of the waterfall seemed to fade from her ears. The sudden kiss of warm sunlight on her skin replaced the chill of the cold damp castle. The unmistakable scent of freshly cut grass invaded her nose.

Am I dreaming?

Amanda opened her eyes. She tried squinting but seemed unable to successfully shield herself from the sun's intensity.

She felt somehow lighter, as if a crushing weight had been lifted. *What was I doing?* She couldn't remember. *Something important.* Her thoughts were scattered as she tried to focus on whatever was happening.

Her view seemed wrong, lower than it should have been. Strands of jet-black hair hung freely around her face instead of the rich, buttery color she knew to be her own.

Legs, too short to be hers, were kicking out in excited anticipation. The metal shackle that circled her ankle was missing. *I'm free*, she thought as she tried to get up and run, but the legs would not obey her as they continued to swing back and forth. Brightly colored sneakers adorned each foot, one with a blue shoelace, the other with red.

Although Amanda could feel the chair beneath her and the muscles working to kick out the legs, she was not in control. *Am I a passenger of some sort?* she wondered. *Have I been projected here somehow? If I have been, why don't I seem to be me?*

It was as if a scene was playing out and she was the main

character, only it wasn't really her at all. It was like she was seeing through someone else's eyes. *Am I?* She tried to blink the vision away.

The scene was focused on the house to the right. A white fence grew from each side, creating an enclosure that surrounded the well-kept yard. A tall woman with equally dark hair carrying a half-filled garbage bag appeared in the door frame.

"Can I open them now? Please..." a young girl's voice begged. Amanda could feel the movement of the jaw as she spoke. Her view shifted to a small pile of unopened gifts that rested on the picnic table before her.

"Your father is going to be so disappointed that he missed the whole thing. Can you be patient so he can watch you open your presents?" the woman said.

"Ughh, can I at least help you pick up?" the girl offered. "It will make it go faster."

"Nonsense! It's your birthday, and you're still my little princess, even if you aren't so little anymore." The woman knelt down beside the girl and tenderly pushed strands of hair away from her face and behind her ear.

"Learning to be patient is important." The woman's eyes twinkled as she caressed the girl's cheek.

Amanda felt the girl's smile widen as she looked up at the woman, her eyes pleading for what she desired.

The woman dropped her hand and stood, picking up the now full trash bag. "Okay, one... pick just one. But wait until I go inside so I can't change my mind," she teased.

As the woman disappeared from view, Amanda was shifted to her feet. Her view moved toward the gifts, scrutinizing them.

A finger pointed out, poking each. "Eeny, meeny, miny, moe..."

In her excitement, the girl hit a gift bag too hard, knocking it from the table. As she bent down to pick it up, the glistening wrapper of another fallen present caught her eye.

She picked up both and plopped the bag back onto the table, her eyes studying the neatly wrapped package. There was no writing on it anywhere. She sat down on the ground, holding the small box, and removed the shiny metallic paper.

A plain cardboard box emerged, and Amanda felt the girl's brow furrow momentarily with disappointment. The child stood up again and held her breath as she lifted the cover from the box.

Amanda was jolted by the sight of the light purple stone that rested inside. It filled her with a sense of unease. The feeling came and went so fast, Amanda forgot what she had even been worried about as she was hit by the girl's intense joy.

Amanda could do nothing but watch as the girl placed it into the palm of her hand. Amanda could feel the girl's pride for her newly acquired treasure emanating through her.

The young girl ran inside quickly, coming up behind her mother, and squeezed her just above the waist.

"Thanks, Mom!"

The woman turned, looking baffled, and hugged back. "Go play outside until your dad gets home."

Obediently, the girl turned back to the door and ran into the yard.

Amanda became dizzy with the movements. *How is it possible to be dizzy in a dream?*

The girl walked along the perimeter of the fence that separated her yard from the next and the next. She came to a stop and placed the stone in her pocket.

Amanda could see the poor creature lying there, blinking slowly on the ground. Amanda could feel it as the girl reached down and scooped it up. Its wing was bent awkwardly, and it didn't fight against the small hand that groped it. Amanda felt a sudden sadness wash over her as the girl inspected the bird with care. She could feel the weak heartbeat of the tiny bird through the girl's touch.

A muted static sound grew around the girl. Amanda could feel the magic crash against her, begging to be released.

The magic Amanda had used in the tomb had felt different. She remembered how the ground had shaken, trembling beneath that power.

This felt as if it was forcing its way out, like an animal that had been caged for too long. *No, don't,* Amanda thought.

Suddenly the girl was hopeful again. It was automatic, like taking a breath. Knowledge that had always been inside, an impulse that had been uncovered. Amanda tried to push that hope away, knock it back, but she couldn't change the girl's feelings any more than she could make the girl walk where she wanted her to.

Amanda felt powerless as she watched the scenario unfold. She knew the girl was experiencing this for the first time. She could feel that it was telling the girl to do it. Urgently begging her to do it, demanding action.

Amanda wanted out. *Out of this dream, this vision, whatever it is.* She knew what was coming. Magic always had a price, and she didn't want to know how this little girl was going to have to pay for it. Amanda was scared for her.

Amanda tried to push the vision away as the girl ran inside, understanding she was going to do something amazing, something that the girl thought her mom would be proud of, something only the girl could do. *People like her are always frightened by what they can't understand or explain away,* Amanda thought, hoping the girl could feel her in the same way she could feel the girl.

"Momma!" the young girl called out.

The woman turned from her chore and peered into the out-stretched hands before her. "Oh Emily, what happened to that poor thing?"

"Watch, Momma!"

Amanda felt it then, the tidal wave of power as it rushed outward over the creature, finally released.

Amanda fought against the vision, trying to will it away. She didn't want to see what came next. She knew something was going to happen, something the girl's mother wouldn't be able to simply explain away. Magic had brought Amanda nothing but heartache in the human plane.

Emily flattened her outstretched hands, and the little bird stood, looking around as it spread its wings and took off, flying over their heads and straight back through the opened door. Emily grinned.

Amanda closed her eyes in defeat. Her fears were confirmed as she felt the sting of the sharp slap that hit the face she was a part of. She felt the girl's sudden shocked confusion toward her mother's actions for being punished over such a great accomplishment.

Amanda opened her eyes to the warm sensation of the tears that welled up in the girl's eyes as the girl looked up at her mother.

Amanda saw the fearful look on the mother's face just as everything went dark and silent.

Slowly, the sound of the waterfall returned to Amanda's ears. She hugged herself against the chill as she acclimated to the coolness of the castle. Stacks of books were piled around the desk where she sat. She tried to shake off the confusion of being thrust into the vision. Reality settled back in around her. She was a prisoner, her only friends helpless against the man that detained them. She had to find some way to free them, but she still felt so powerless.

Amanda pushed the encounter out of her mind, suddenly annoyed by the intrusion and the memories it caused to resurface. She had other things to take care of. She wouldn't be a help to anyone if she couldn't help herself.

She reached for the book that lay open on the floor, again studying the runes on the cover.

She remembered where she had seen them before. *The forest.* The place where her nightmare had truly begun. She angrily threw the book with as much strength as she could muster straight at the wall, knocking half a shelf of texts to the floor.

Amanda forced herself to grab a different book, trying to continue the research, determined to find some kind of solution, but the wall she had carefully constructed around her past had been broken and memories continued to pour in.

As she read on, she giggled to herself. The sorcerer had said he caused Erol's imprisonment. It was all starting to make some horrific sense to her. There was nothing left to do but laugh. Aden's capture was the reason for Erol's imprisonment. Erol had purposely kept the truth from her. She felt sick to her stomach. Her heart ached, her chest felt heavy. She wanted to cry, but she couldn't; there was nothing left to cry for.

Her mind danced with the realization. *Why would he keep that from me? To save himself?* Amanda's hands trembled. She balled them into fists to stop their uncontrollable movement.

She let anger take over as she devised her plan to get the ring and secure her freedom.

18

"Are you prepared for what you have to do?" Jacob said, looking deeply into Amanda's eyes.

Amanda grinned slyly. "Yes, and I am looking forward to it." She poked his chest. "Are you sure you're ready for what's coming?" She turned to walk away.

Jacob grabbed at her hand and pulled her back toward him. "Your eyes have changed color." His smile widened as he released his hold. "This will never do. Sit." He pointed to the uncomfortable chair she had spent so many hours in. A small silver mirror lay on the desk, and she lifted it in front of her face. Amanda gasped at her reflection as unfamiliar deep red eyes stared back at her.

The sorcerer pushed a stray piece of Amanda's hair from her face. "Shh, my puppet, relax. Don't you trust me?"

Jacob waved his hand over her face as he spoke, casting an enchantment over her eyes. Amanda lifted the mirror, inspecting his work. She loosened her grip on the mirror as she was met by her familiar blue eyes. "Thank you."

Amanda stood and placed her hand in Jacob's so he could lead her away.

Amanda called to Erol as soon as she was back in her room. She put her arms around him and pulled him close. He barely tried to struggle as her lips brushed against his. He gave in then and kissed her back; it was a hard, passionate kiss of a kind she had never felt before. Her heart pounded against her chest. *Do it.*

A shiver ran down her spine as she reached behind her and gripped the iron knife that was tucked into the back of her skirt. *It's the only way.* She pressed herself into him even more, not letting him come up for air. *Why doesn't he resist?* In one quick movement, she shoved the iron into his human-shaped spine.

Erol gasped and collapsed to the floor, and as Amanda had expected, he disappeared. Quickly, she wiped the strange-looking black blood from the knife onto her eyes. Then she threw the blade to the floor where Erol had been just a moment before.

She crumpled, taking slow, heavy breaths. *What have I done?* Amanda shook her head and pulled herself back up into standing position. *It was the only way.*

"Was that necessary?" Aden materialized beside her.

Was it? Amanda asked herself as she stared at the place he had landed. "The blood?" she whispered. "So that jinn can no longer hide from my vision. That's the theory, anyway," she added, still staring.

"Ready?" *Am I?* Amanda wondered, knowing Aden had been there all along. Watching, waiting. Amanda crossed her arms over her chest as a shiver ran through her.

She felt Aden slide his arm around her waist and let him lead her into the wind. She couldn't get the image of Erol out of her mind. *I must continue, there's no turning back.*

It seemed that they traveled a long time; instead of stepping through like she had with Erol, it felt almost like she was flying. The wind seemed to swirl around them as they moved. Then the wind changed direction, and suddenly she felt dizzy and sick. As they landed, she gulped the air and steadied herself.

Amanda turned in a circle to take in the rare view of the mountains that encircled this portion of the spirit realm. From peak to base they glinted and sparkled as if they truly were embedded with emeralds, just as the books had described. The very ground beneath her feet seemed to vibrate and hum with their magic.

The valley was filled with lush vegetation; large red flowers dotted the landscape. The remnants of a long abandoned village rose in the far distance in one direction. The dilapidated thatched-roof homes barely seemed to be standing.

Curious, Amanda looked for a path that would lead toward the ruined village. Aden clasped her hand.

"Amanda." He paused after each word. "Don't." He looked into her eyes, pleading with her. "Please..." His eyes seemed to be filled with sorrow.

Amanda shrugged. "Fine." She could understand not wanting to be reminded of the past. *Needing not to be reminded.* Amanda looked down at her hands, trembling slightly.

The place seems deserted anyway. Leery that her spell hadn't worked, she wondered if there would have been another way out of this. She stroked the diamond in her pocket for courage. *No other way out.*

At least Erol no longer has to suffer.

As the texts had promised, a lone dark tower loomed in the opposite direction far in the distance.

They walked hand in hand through the fields, like they both had every right to be there. Something blue whizzed past Amanda's face and down into the overgrown vegetation, startling her. *The wisps?* Amanda grinned as she looked around for the mysterious creatures.

"Amanda, what are you looking for?"

"I thought I saw something." Amanda dropped to her knees in the grass beside some of the bright red flowers. She brushed at the palm-sized petals with her hand, parting them to inspect the area closer to the ground. "I swore it went past by my face, a blue creature, it swooped down and I thought…"

A red thing unfolded itself from one of the petals and darted at her. Angry at the intrusion, it circled her head once, flapping its leathery wings.

Then, as if cursing at her, it stopped, hovering directly in front of her face, its small claws poised for attack if necessary as it took in the sight of her.

She could see its tiny nostrils flare as the small winged reptile opened its mouth, releasing a puff of smoke. It beat its wings in her direction one more time as if making a point before turning and flying away, its long slender tail whipping back and forth behind it.

Aden lowered himself to sit by Amanda.

Amanda leaned in closer to the ground and watched as another similar creature uncurled itself from the deep grass, this one an identical shade of green. It spread its wings and beat them several times, revealing sharp spikes that lined its back before it lifted and flew away.

Aden grinned. "Dragons." She raised one eyebrow and stood, placing her hands on her hips. "In human lore that's what they call them, anyway." Aden continued to examine the shrubbery.

"No way, those are tiny."

"They always were." Aden looked up at her, squinting as the sun hit his eyes. "Humans have a tendency to embellish, from what I have learned, anyway." He went back to his search. "They come in all sorts of colors, and they are very protective of their homes."

Amanda watched him as he hunted. For a moment he looked happy. His eyes seemed to twinkle with excitement.

Aden stood back up. "I had always wanted to see them up close. They never used to come down from their mountain nests..." He stumbled over the words, adding, "When I was a youngling." Aden's eyes glazed over, and his frown returned.

"They are kind of cute." Amanda smirked again. "Can they be blue?" she added, remembering what she had been looking for to begin with, still hoping it had been a wisp. She hadn't seen them anywhere in the castle since she had left the dungeon.

Aden nodded. "They like to rest where they can blend in, like camouflage. They may be cute, but their claws and teeth are razor-sharp." Aden made a scratching motion with his hand and cocked his head. "Don't worry, like I said, their nests are high up in the mountains, hidden in cracks and crevasses. They won't attack unless you disturb those."

"Well," Amanda reached her hand out to Aden, "we will be sure to stay away from the mountain range then."

As they got closer, the tower reflected light off its dark surface as if it had been meticulously polished and shined. There appeared to be no gaps or breaks in the spire that seemed to rise forever above them, like it had been formed from one singular piece of rock.

As the entrance came into full view, Amanda could see a man with what looked like smooth, scaly skin seated on the ground in front of it. She clutched the gem for courage, reminding herself that jinn could come in all shapes and sizes, and some had control over their appearance. Aden gave her other hand a tight squeeze before releasing his grip.

The serpent-like jinn waved his arm, shooing away a few dragons that had been resting on him. Amanda looked at Aden, raising her eyebrows.

Aden shrugged. "I guess the guardian was lonely," he whispered. "It explains why the dragons weren't worried about coming down from the mountains."

The dragons are his only companions. How long has he been here all alone? Amanda thought of the wisps and how they had visited her in the dungeon. If she could have transformed herself to draw them from wherever it was they lived and get them to stay, she would have. *You need to do this. You have to save Aden and yourself.* She took in a deep breath. *What if it's too late to save me?* Amanda's thoughts were broken as the guardian spoke.

"Why have you come here?" The guardian's voice was raspy, and he let out a serpent-like hiss at the end of his sentence. Amanda tightened her grip on the stone in her pocket and exhaled.

"I have come to collect my reward for freeing this jinni from a sorcerer," Amanda announced, gesturing toward Aden with her free hand.

The guardian stood, towering over her and Aden. "And how am I supposed to believe you freed him from one we have searched centuries for, when we could not?"

Amanda caught sight of their shadow-like reflections on the tower wall. She looked so small compared to the jinn. She forced herself to stand up taller and peered into the guardian's serpent-like eyes. "The sorcerer kidnapped me. When I learned the secret of his stone dagger, I bided my time, waiting for him to trust me."

The guardian remained motionless, staring back into her gaze. Amanda had to stop herself from looking away as she continued.

"When I was finally allowed access to the dagger, I melted the iron seal from it, releasing him for all time." The lie stung as it flowed from her mouth. She remained focused on his vertical pupils and concentrated on keeping her words steady.

The jinn took one step toward her as he opened his mouth to speak. "And how, my dear, have you found your way here?" He motioned around himself. "Even with the help of this jinni, it should not be possible."

Amanda frowned as she exposed her shoulders to him. His jaw went slack at the sight of the carvings. "What is your request?"

"I request the knowledge of the ring."

The jinn let out a hiss at the mention of the ring. "That is a large request coming from someone so small." The hair on Amanda's arms prickled as the guardian let out another hiss.

"Oh, am I really so small?" Amanda's palms felt sweaty as she gripped the stone.

"Yessss," the jinn bellowed as the air swirled between them. His body began to stretch and widen before her eyes. *Don't move.* Amanda clenched her teeth and tried to dig her shoes into the dirt as the guardian grew to be seven feet tall right in front of her eyes.

Amanda unclenched her jaw, and a sly smile spread across her face. "Oh wow, I am minuscule compared to that." She walked around the guardian as if examining him from head to toe. "It is too bad you can only get bigger," Amanda said, knowing how much jinn liked to show off and counting on it. "I mean, no disrespect." She giggled. "It's just that we grow every day, do we not?" She stopped in front of him, again meeting his eyes.

"I can get so small, you would never find me, even if you held the blade of grass in which I was on in your hand," the jinn retorted.

Amanda rolled her eyes and placed her hands on her hips. "I doubt that," she countered, reaching down to pluck a blade from the ground and twirling it between her fingers.

"I will show you." He snorted, too preoccupied to see that Aden now held Erol's old prison in his hands.

Amanda felt the air swirl in front of her again as he began to transform, slowly shrinking down until he finally disappeared from view.

Aden moved beside her and held out the prison. Amanda didn't remove her eyes from the blade of grass that she held between her fingers, waiting.

The blade bounced down and sprang back up, indicating the guardian had landed on it. Amanda began reciting the special words she had memorized from the book.

Just as the strange runes began to glow, Aden lifted the lid and Amanda placed the blade of grass with the jinn on it inside and replaced the lid, trapping him.

Amanda took the prison in both hands. As the glow faded, she rubbed the runes along its side.

Light green smoke billowed out of the lamp as the guardian appeared before them. "You don't know what you have set in motion!" he screamed, even before his form had time to solidify.

"I command you to tell me the hiding place of the ring," Amanda growled.

"The ring was destroyed to keep it from the hands of evil." He looked at Amanda. "And you. Jacob has sent you on a wild goose chase." The guardian looked at the ground, moving his head from side to side.

Amanda's eyes became slits as she regarded the guardian. "It's not possible." She pointed her finger in his face. "You're lying."

The guardian looked up at her, a thin smile spreading on his lips. "We can't lie when we are imprisoned in this way. Didn't your servant teach you that? We may withhold information, but we cannot lie." The guardian turned toward Aden. "And you. You are not even free, are you?" Aden looked away from the newly trapped being. Amanda dug her nails into her hand as the guardian continued. "Think, Amanda." He pointed to his temple. "Maybe Jacob just got exactly what he wanted."

Amanda felt her face grow hot.

"A pawn, Amanda, you were a pawn in his twisted game."

Her heart pounded. "Get back in there."

The guardian shrugged. "Fine, what worse could you possibly do to me?"

As the guardian dispersed and reentered his prison, a snarl escaped Amanda's lips.

"Let's leave this place." She reached for Aden's hand and yanked him close. A new cruel smile danced on her face as she envisioned an even better punishment. She clutched the prison with her free hand, holding it tightly.

As Amanda and Aden traveled together, she reached out into the void and then let go of the prison, allowing it to drop into the unknown.

19

Amanda waited for Jacob, pacing the stone floor of the library. What had she done? She had played right into Jacob's expectations.

When they returned to the castle, Aden didn't say a word to her about the fate of the guardian. Her face had been wet with tears. He had lifted her chin and nodded. "If you're going to do something, now is the time to strike. Jacob thinks he has broken you." Amanda tried to look away, but he held her face, forcing her to look into his eyes. "Don't tell me what you plan to do. It's better, safer, if I don't know." He planted a light kiss on her cheek and released her chin. I know you're strong enough." Then he had left her to wait alone.

"Ah, you have returned at last," Jacob said as he entered the room. "And more powerful than ever." He rubbed his hands together. "Aren't you glad I helped you realize your potential?"

She shook her head, still pacing. "Why, why, why!" She screamed the last word out, spitting in his face.

"You know of course, dearest, deep down." He grinned, wiping her spit from his cheek. "What's the point of being the most powerful sorcerer and to live forever when the only company I have is this ungrateful jinni?" he said, gesturing to Aden. "Why are you joining us this evening, anyway, ifrit?"

Amanda hadn't seen Aden return, and she looked up to meet

his eyes. He nodded once in her direction before looking down at his feet.

"I want him here," Amanda responded.

"Fine," Jacob said, shrugging. "Are you going to be a problem or a solution? I mean, I can't complain. You have already helped me so much, what with you destroying Erol and all."

Amanda's face paled. "I released him; I didn't destroy him."

"Whatever helps you sleep at night." He grabbed her arm, squeezing painfully. "You realize he caused all of this." She nodded.

"I have heard the story, mostly," Amanda said. Looking away from him, she breathed in deeply, her fingers grazing the black jewel in her pocket. *Maybe.* She breathed deeply, considering her options.

"Unlocking your power was a rather delightful bonus during the whole escapade." He smiled. "I have helped you become who you really are. Your true nature would have shown through. Eventually. I just hastened the process." *My power?* Amanda removed the stone from her pocket and held it in her hand. *He doesn't know about the stone.*

"You did, didn't you," Amanda said, looking down at the stone. She had to finish what she started. "I am grateful." She looked up at him and forced a weak smile.

"Good," he said smugly. "I wish only for you to understand what you're truly capable of." He took a step toward her and placed a hand on her shoulder.

"Thank you," Amanda said as he inspected her.

His eyes lit up with curiosity as he surveyed the stone she held. "Where did you get that?"

"It was a gift," Amanda said, turning it in her hand. "You know, someone told me black diamonds grant courage. It is said they allow a person to look within without illusion."

"Poppycock," the sorcerer said, shaking his head.

"You're right, you know, it hasn't seemed to work for me very well." The diamond glinted in the candlelight. "They also said it could be used to amplify magical energies. But I wouldn't even know how to go about doing something like that." She shrugged and pretended to inspect the flawless gem. She looked up at Jacob. "You wouldn't be interested in a trade, would you?" She looked back down at the gem, shaking her head. "No, of course not, what would a powerful sorcerer need such a silly trinket for."

"Trade?" He scratched thoughtfully at his beard. Amanda could feel the magic pushing at her, and she focused on allowing a tiny amount to escape. The stones beneath her feet vibrated. *Steady, just enough to make Jacob curious.* She pulled back the magic and looked up at Jacob as if nothing had happened. "Your wonderful dagger. I understand it was of your own design. I wish to take a closer look at it, to study your impressive craftsmanship." Amanda cocked her head at him and raised her eyebrows.

Jacob continued to scratch his chin. "My dagger is rather remarkable, isn't it." He chewed at his lip as he looked at the stone. "I guess it couldn't hurt, maybe just on a temporary basis."

"Sure." She shrugged. "Although I'm sure it wouldn't be of any real use to someone like you."

"Aden, bring what Amanda requests." Amanda's mouth curled in a thin smile.

Aden nodded. "As you wish."

"Amanda," Jacob beamed, "I'm glad you have decided to take a real interest in the arcane arts. You will find that you, that we, can accomplish amazing things together."

Amanda forced her smile to spread. "Yes." Her eyes gleamed with the excitement of what she was about to do. "I think we really can."

As Aden returned with the dagger and sheath, Amanda tossed the gem toward Jacob.

Jacob reached for the diamond, but as it met his flesh, he pulled away in pain, quickly dropping it to the floor. "What is the meaning of this?" His face was crimson; his eyes grew wide as Aden handed Amanda the dagger. Jacob backed up a few steps. "It's too late, Amanda. We, together, have set things into motion. Things that you can't even fathom. Everything is about to change."

"Then why do you sound so scared?" Amanda turned the dagger in her empty hand, examining it. She walked toward Jacob and snatched up the diamond from the floor.

Amanda clutched the black diamond in one hand and the dagger in the other, willing the seal to break. She moved her mouth into a crooked smile. *At least I managed to make it the truth it in the end. That has to count for something.*

The sorcerer's grin returned. "Killing me," he motioned to Aden, "releasing the ifrit, will change nothing." He growled. "The world will go back to how it was meant to be, and you can't stop it."

Amanda could hear a slight tremble in his voice at the end, and it exhilarated her. *He really is scared of me.* She pushed more of the strange magic toward him; the castle began to shake, as the walls had in the burial chamber.

Shelves tilted and fell from the wall; books flew about the room as if caught in a tornado. Frightened, the sorcerer backed up and started to chant.

Free from Jacob's hold, Aden advanced on him before he

could complete the spell, pushing him down with his own jinn magic, paralyzing him. Amanda stood over the top of the Arcane sorcerer, and her smile grew. "You wished to unlock my power?" She could feel the magic as it coursed through her veins. "Maybe you should be more careful about what you wish for." She winked down at his cowering form as she began to chant in the secret language of the Arcane sorcerers, stripping him of his magical abilities and poisoning his mind.

20

Amanda sat in her tower room staring at herself in the closet mirror. Without the aid of Jacob's magic, her eyes again were red. She squinted at her reflection. *I really do look like my mother.* She didn't flinch as she felt Aden's hand caress her shoulder. She kept her eyes straight ahead as she spoke. "You will be leaving now?"

He lowered himself and sat beside her. "Leaving?"

"To go back to your family." Amanda looked down at her lap. Aden reached for her chin and forced her to look up at him.

"I have no family to go back to, Amanda. They ran. You saw the village. It was long deserted."

"Still, you're free." She turned away. "I can never go back to that life after the things I have done, the things I have seen."

"Amanda, you did what you had to do to free yourself. You freed us all in one way or another."

"I don't feel free." Amanda wrung her hands together. "I have no one to go back to."

"You have me."

She turned sharply back to him, a tear rolling down her cheek. "I killed him, Aden."

Aden reached toward her and gently wiped the tear away. "Jacob's alive. I released him in a remote forest of the human realm. He will wander around mumbling like a lunatic for the rest of his days."

"Erol," she choked out.

"He wanted to be freed, Amanda. Don't you think he would have done something to stop you?" Amanda stood and walked to the tiny slit of a window. "You have nothing to be ashamed of. You did what you had to do to survive." Amanda continued to peer out at the water that cascaded down, distorting the world beyond. "My capture wasn't the only thing Erol had been keeping from you." Amanda turned back to him. "Amanda, what do you know of your mother?"

She hugged her arms to her chest. "Not much. I don't see what that has to do with anything."

"Jacob had been keeping an eye on Erol's prison for centuries without making a move." Aden stood. "Jacob knew you had something different coursing through your veins the moment you stumbled into the woods. That's why he sent me to find out more. I'm not sure what his exact plan was once he found out your mother came from the demon realm, but it was never to get the ring."

"Demon?" Amanda held her hands out in front of her, studying them. "My mother wasn't evil." She thought of the half-ruined book Jacob had given her; it had said that demons could harness shadows. Remembering how the magic had been so strong that first time, in the gloom-filled tomb and then again when she had attacked Jacob in the shadow-filled library, it made sense. *But it can't be true.* The book had also said that the demons and the Arcane were both created by the goddess Mia. *Would that make me a natural enemy of the jinn?* Amanda pushed the thought away as Aden spoke.

"Demons aren't inherently evil, Amanda, that's a fallacy. They simply are another type of being created by the goddesses and given the ability to harness dark magic. As far as I can tell, from the information your father had and Jacob could find, Fatin was summoned with powerful magic by the humans of the west to stop your father's team from unearthing something."

"So what you're telling me is that my father lied to me! Is there anyone that didn't keep secrets from me?" Amanda's arms went to her sides. She clenched her fists.

"I can't tell you if he knew." Aden looked at his feet. "That secret died with him."

"And Erol." Amanda's heart pounded in her chest.

"Bloise told him and made him promise to reveal the truth."

Amanda furrowed her brow. "And you?"

"I was unable to speak of it, Jacob made sure of that. He wanted your abilities to manifest on their own. The gem was something he hadn't seen coming."

"The black diamond..."

"Obviously it's no ordinary black diamond... I don't think Erol knew when he gave it to you. Do you know where he got it from?"

Amanda shook her head. "It appeared out of thin air, but..."

"Everything comes from somewhere, Amanda."

"The jinni in the tomb knew something."

"Well then, let's find her."

"I wouldn't know where to start."

Aden reached for her hand and gripped it firmly. "We will search together." Amanda squeezed back and followed him into the wind.

Epilogue: Emily

There had been no warning,

Emily sat with her back resting against her bedroom door. Black, curly hair hung over her face like a barricade as she examined her hands, her chin almost touching her chest.

In books there's always an omen. A sudden onset of stomach pain or gloomy, rain-filled skies.

Emily reached up and gently touched her cheek. Her face still felt hot where her mother's hand had made contact.

Her mother had never spoken to her like that before, had never hit her before.

There had been no warning.

The sun had been shining. The sky had been clear. No clouds of any type had been apparent before or after. It had been an exceptionally beautiful day, and Emily could still see bright sunlight coming in through her small bedroom window.

How could what I did be a bad thing?

She looked down at her shoes; the red lace on the left hung untied. *Why didn't I double-knot it, like the right shoelace?* The bright blue one that hadn't tripped her up as she hurried away from her mother and up the stairs, her heart pounding, her face stinging.

She knew it wasn't normal, the thing she did, but wasn't it a good thing, a beautiful thing? Emily wrapped a strand of her hair around her finger.

It had felt right. It had felt wonderful to push the wave over the bird and watch it fly away.

A tightness had formed in her chest afterward, and it lingered there, waiting. *Waiting for what?* Emily had tried to push it out, like the wave over the bird, but nothing happened.

Daddy will be home soon. He will make it right.

Emily crawled over to her window and looked out into the street. Everything outside still seemed the same as always. Normal. Two silver garbage cans sat at the end of the driveway, awaiting morning pickup. Neighbors waved to one another as they passed on the sidewalk. A small girl played with a jump rope across the street.

Emily watched as her mother appeared, heading toward the garbage cans, a full bag in hand. She could see colorful wrapping paper though the clear plastic as her mother lifted the lid and stuffed the bag inside. Emily squinted to try to see exactly what its contents were, but it was no use. She was too far away.

Her mother greeted a jogger with a smile and a wave before turning on her heels to reenter the house.

Normal, Emily thought again as she moved to return to her spot against the door.

The sun had disappeared before Emily heard the creak of one step, and then another as someone made their way up toward her room at the top of the staircase.

Emily could hear a sniffling noise outside the door.

"Momma?" Emily turned and rested her hand on the door. "Momma, can I come out now?"

A bag rustled and metal clinked on the other side. She heard her mother clear her throat.

"Momma?" Emily's eyes grew wide as she heard a whirring, buzzing noise.

"Momma, talk to me!" The tightness in her chest grew. She yelled, pounding her fist against the wood. "Please!"

The buzzing stopped and the bag rustled again. "Please," she whispered this time as a static sound filled her ears.

She heard the newly installed lock click into place.

"You're unnatural, you don't belong here." The wave of pressure expelled from her chest.

Her mother screamed. Emily heard a familiar thud as something hit the stair railing.

Emily reached for her doorknob and tugged at it, yelling, "Momma, are you okay?"

Something banged against her door, and Emily jumped back.

"Don't you dare call me that," her mother screeched.

Emily crumpled back to the floor. She heard the stairs creak as her mother made a slow descent.

Fresh tears streamed down her cheeks, and she curled herself into a ball, her shoulders trembling as she whispered, "I will be good, I swear."

Something tickled the side of her face, and Emily swatted at it.

She sat up and rubbed her puffy eyes. Three blue balls of light hovered in front of her. Emily reached out toward them, and her fingers tingled as they passed through the wispy blue creatures.

Book Two

Emily thinks her parents will be proud of her when she reveals a magic trick to them on her birthday. After all, Emily was taught that people's differences are what make them beautiful. But when she shows her parents just how unique she is they withdraw from her, afraid of the thing she can do.

For years Emily has endured her parent's harsh treatment without her curse showing itself. But when her best friend has an accident, she cannot ignore the compulsion to save her. Afraid to return to her home, Emily wanders struggling to survive on her own in a dangerous world where trouble and magic seem to follow her everywhere she goes.

Her journey leads her to a small town unlike any she has come to before. Just as Emily comes to terms with the town's secret, clan members start disappearing. Something is threatening the peace of the Jinn refuge. Emily vows to discover and stop the force that is behind the destruction of the one place where she felt that she could finally belong.

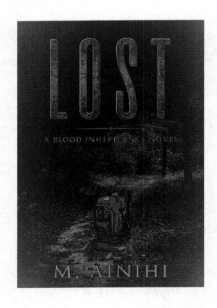

To learn more about The Blood Inheritance Quartet visit: https://mainihi.wordpress.com

About The Author

M. Ainihi is a passionate YA Dark Fantasy Author, proud Mother, Wife, and Adventurer. Hailing from the wilds of Upstate New York and currently residing in the Chicagoland area, Rise is her first novel in a planned quartet.

Made in the USA
Lexington, KY
15 December 2018